S0-CWR-740

Sixkiller stood between the two aliens, his back pressed against the floater; he appeared to be trying to protect expeditionary property from a threat still not wholly clear to him. His eyes—Keiko saw when they were nearer—were wide with apprehension and resolve.

Andrik turned to Keiko's student, who was suddenly the same height as the human beings, its posture both poised and expectant. "What is the Rite of Conjoining?" the xenologist asked. "Just before everyone down there," gesturing towards the crater, "froze up on us again, we were invited to attend a ceremony by that name."

"Yes, do come. At Onogoro's decoupling."

"But what is it?"

"A sharing of data preparatory to transit. A celebration of conceptions. An obeisance to the forces of delivery."

"It has to do with birth then?"

"Birth, resurrection, renewal, and life—all at strata of consciousness inaccessible to the unconjoined."

"Then how the hell are we going to participate?" Sixkiller demanded. "Do we bring our own extension cords and plug into the nearest faintly humming Kyber?"

The Kyber tore off a piece of flesh from its right arm and offered it to Sixkiller. "Eat thou this in remembrance of what thou hast never been," it said, not untenderly.

UNDER HEAVEN'S BRIDGE

UNDER HEAVEN'S BRIDGE

MICHAEL BISHOP
& IAN WATSON

SF
ace books
A Division of Charter Communications Inc.
A GROSSET & DUNLAP COMPANY
51 Madison Avenue
New York, New York 10010

UNDER HEAVEN'S BRIDGE

Copyright © 1981 by Ian Watson and Michael Bishop

All rights reserved. No part of this book may be reproduced in any form or by any means, except for the inclusion of brief quotations in a review, without permission in writing from the publisher.

All characters in this book are fictitious. Any resemblance to actual persons, living or dead, is purely coincidental.

An ACE Book
First American Edition
Published by arrangement with Victor Gollancz Ltd., London

First Ace printing: April 1982
Published Simultaneously in Canada

2 4 6 8 0 9 7 5 3 1
Manufactured in the United States of America

To Greg Benford

PROLOGUE

On the fifteenth of January, two weeks before Keiko's eighth birthday, the Takahashi family travelled in to the centre of Kyoto on the electric railway from their home in the southern suburb of Fushimi Ward. Young Keiko was dressed in a particularly bright red and white kimono, which made her something of an exotic butterfly, untimely hatched in January.

She watched, agog, while the gold-tiled pagoda citadels of Momoyama Castle slipped into the distance, along with the adjacent funfair: space shuttles swinging round a high, cantilever-armed pylon. Then the tree-clad hill behind the Inari Shrine briefly loomed and receded, specked with drops of vermilion blood—some of the many lacquered stone gateways that climbed it, to be replaced as a landmark by the ugly spike of Kyoto Tower. Staring outward from the rocking, crowded train, Keiko ignored the myriad close-packed houses and workshops between the shrine and the tower. She had eyes only for her destination—while Mrs. Takahashi had eyes only for her, in her butterfly array.

Keiko's older brother and sister were wearing their ordinary black school uniforms today: soldiers in the army of education. Indeed, brother Okido *was* martially inclined, having already won a yellow belt in kendo though only twelve years old—which was the nominal reason why the Takahashis were travelling in to town, to watch the traditional archery contest that lasted from morning till evening in the grounds of Sanjusangendo, the long hall that measured out the range. They had been to see the contest the previous January, and Keiko, bored, had strayed away into the hall itself . . .

Each time the train went *cluck-cluck* over the rail joints Okido drew back his arm and, with a quick whoosh of breath, sent an imaginary arrow flying over the grey tiled roofs. Sister Etsuko, a rather fat girl, admired him blatantly. Mr Takahashi frowned, admittedly more as though he was judging each shot rather than rebuking the boy's high spirits. When his glance fell upon Keiko though—their flower—his face would melt, and he would smile self-indulgently.

After leaving the train they walked the few blocks to Sanjusangendo where, in the white-pebble precinct, archers young and old—shoulders and breasts bared like Amazons'—pulled back their high bowstrings and let fly, again and again and again. The archers were watched in turn, and filmed, by four or five hundred spectators, busily holo-freezing hundreds of times the same ancient poses—just as, inside the hall itself, mused Keiko, was reproduced a thousand times . . .

She held her thought, as one holds a breath before plunging underwater into another world with inhabitants different from ours.

"The record for all times," bragged Okido, "never bested since, was set over four hundred years ago—"

By a samurai who fired more than thirteen thousand arrows, more than eight thousand of which covered the full distance from one end of the hall to the other. Keiko shook her head. If you multiplied the numbers, had that famous samurai fired an arrow as far as the Moon? It meant nothing to her. The figures were an empty chant. Whereas in the hall itself . . . numbers were another matter.

Hwit! . . . *Thuck!* Another arrow flew, another, another. Holocameras pointed everywhere.

At this point a foreign man and his wife sidled up to the Takahashis through the crowd of spectators. The man was beefy-faced, with curly ginger hair—a kind of demon, dressed in a blue parka, like an inflated tent. His wife a stout black woman, wore bulky white furs against the January chill.

"Please," said the man in phrasebook Japanese, atrociously pronounced, pointing a mittened finger at little Keiko. "Beautiful. Picture?" He was a monstrous *gaijin*—an outside person, an alien. The notion of aliens was speculatively in the news these days, now that humanity was heading out to the stars from Luna Base. Was this creature any less alien than some star-monster?

While Mr Takahashi wondered what the foreigner was saying, and Mrs Takahashi hid giggles behind her hand, nothing was said in reply. Not until Keiko herself piped up, in textbook English which she pronounced surprisingly well: "Please take picture, sir."

As she posed, Keiko thought what a great thing it might be to speak to aliens. Why, she had just done so! Perhaps they might speak properly in their own languages, however preposterously they spoke Japanese.

The meaty, tent-clad *gaijin* beamed, showing what seemed like rows and rows of teeth. Mr Takahashi nodded, and the alien touched a button on its camera.

"Why, thank you, little girl!" the creature boomed.

Shortly after this, Keiko saw her chance and slipped away. For the moment she had forgotten about the red-faced alien waving its box of frozen memories.

She made her way round to the entrance of the hall, well out of arrow range. Her father might be annoyed, but he would forgive, and very quickly too. She went in. Here was what she had been waiting for a year to see . . .

ONE

She had the idea that what had attracted her to Andrik Norn, their party's outspoken xenologist, was the intensity with which he lived. Although fast approaching forty, he ignited new enthusiasms daily, like a pyromaniac teenager—or a phoenix, perpetually rising from its own ashes. Andrik burned. He ate, drank, worked, screwed, and even slept—as he was doing now, his trembling eyelids betraying the turbulence of his dreams—with a bleak and impatient gusto.

Sometimes it seemed to Keiko that Andrik had attained the sort of false spiritual liberation that comes from ignoring rather than transcending the self, but even this peculiarly Western aberration, in Andrik, appealed to her—it was so at odds with her own upbringing and values. Leaning down to kiss the sleeping man's forehead, she realized that she loved him.

Still, she was empty of desire.

And why not? Less than an hour ago Andrik and she had sated the demands of the flesh in each other's arms.

Her want of desire had another cause, however. A rather frightening cause. While caressing her lover's shoulder blades, wide-eyed in animal appreciation of the immemorial act, she had suddenly begun to believe that her fingers were moving over . . . not flesh, but hot metal. A small, sick fear had automatically tightened her belly and womb. It was as if one of the clockwork-mannequin Kybers that they had been trying to study here on Onogoro had come out of its death-sleep long enough to possess Andrik's body in order to possess hers.

A wicked, maybe even unnatural, analogy for her to draw. But the xenologist's love-making, usually passionate and adept, had tonight suggested to her the mechanical rather than the carnal.

She forgave Andrik this not uncommon masculine failing, of course, but she could not help wondering if some unholy transubstantiation of flesh to metal were taking place in him because of the sheer intensity of his commitment to researching the Kybers. Notwithstanding his many minor and peripheral interests they were, after all, his overmastering enthusiasm—by personal choice as well as by mission directive. Inasmuch as she, too, had already played an indispensable role in puzzling the enigma of the aliens, maybe her own imagination was to blame for seeing her lover as a machine. Was it possible that her new-found love of Andrik had prompted in her a corrosive jealousy of an entire alien species?

Keiko Takahashi shook her head and smiled. No, certainly not. She was the least likely of all of them to nurture a stupid jealousy of the Kybers. Her fear came from . . . well, the latent anxiety that just being around such mysterious intelligences produced in everybody. The strangeness of living on another world was also a factor, and the research/reconnaissance party from the transnational light-skimmer *Heavenbridge* had been surfaceside for better than two Earth-standard months now, inhabiting the great prefabricated Expeditionary Platform erected for them by the engineers of the exploratory vessel that had discovered the planet a year ago.

It was an unsettling thing, Keiko reflected, having to lie down on a collapsible bedstead in an inflatadorm atop an immense, five-legged scaffold on a world as totally *other* as Onogoro. Even after nearly fifty-five of the planet's long local days, time in which to become reoriented, it was still a disconcerting and anxious-making experience. And now that Onogoro was swinging out of its ellipse around Dextro-Gemini (currently the nearer of its two suns), falling temperatures and weirdly discoloured skies heightened the strangeness. Even the most stolid expedition members had shown signs of tripping brain-over-butts into neuroses. If Keiko's only symptom to date was having briefly taken Andrik's pistoning body for that of a Kyber, well, she was lucky, wasn't she?

Her kiss had not awakened the man. He slept on, not with a baby's deep peacefulness but with a fitful succession of squints and grimaces. What could he be dreaming about, anyway?

Keiko—homesick for Earth, for Kyoto in the spring—eased herself away from Andrik and off the narrow bedstead. Despite the sun-bulb in the ceiling and the heat vents in the walls, the dormicle was chilly. Keiko pulled on a thigh-length robe rather like an abbreviated kimono. Cool air continued to massage her legs, and this not unpleasant stimulus reminded her that there was something in her dresser-file she wanted to take out and examine—but Andrik's descending seed forced her to grab up her discarded singlet and press it to the inside of her thighs.

Seed.

The word—even the substance itself—was reassuring. It absolved Andrik of any taint of mechanicalness. Machines, after all, represented in their bloodless design, manufacture, and function the very opposite of what Andrik's semen meant. Surely in matters of love it was not wrong to be a Luddite. No woman—nor man, either—wanted to embrace a robot.

And yet Keiko remembered that before setting out on this expedition she had spent several days in her own country making nostalgic pilgrimages to the shrines and temples so important to her in her girlhood. Was metal truly devoid of sensation? Was gold genuinely inanimate? Her desire to rummage in her dresser-file for a memento of her youth had arisen from a vivid mental picture of the interior of Sanjusangendo, the renowned Buddhist Hall of Mercy in her native Kyoto.

That temple—a national treasure even in these days of uneasy transnationalism—housed in serried ranks a thousand wooden statues brilliantly alchemized by gold leaf and haloed with radiating aerial spikes. Avatars of Kannon, bodhisattva of Mercy and Compassion, they were important now because she had always felt the utmost awe and reverence in their presence . . . even though it was only lifeless statuary.

Indeed, they were pertinent now because in several disquieting ways the statues of Kannon reminded her of the stilt-walking Kybers of Onogoro. A strange equation . . .

Keiko crossed her dormicle, knelt before her plastic dresser-file, and searched its bottom drawer for the folder containing her modest holofiche collection. Finding it, she smiled in anticipation. Then she went to the desk near the bedstead, inserted the proper card in her holofiche projector, and turned the machine so that the microimages on the card would spring to full-blown life in the holoniche opposite her bed.

A moment later, having slid past several exterior shots of the temple and its grounds (the grand hall, the hanging lanterns on the walk, the rock gardens), Keiko was gazing across ten staggered rows of the beautiful gilded statues of the bodhisattva. Her dormicle, miraculously transmuted, was now as spacious and serene as the fabled Hall of Mercy itself.

Overcome, Keiko wept.

TWO

Keiko Takahashi was the mission's linguist and data specialist, in which latter role she functioned as both librarian and archivist. This yoking of specialties had influenced her selection to the research/reconnaissance team taking passage aboard the *Heavenbridge* from Luna Port and heading out to the Gemini system and the anomalous little planet orbiting Dextro. Officially the world was called, altogether unimaginatively, Dextro-Gemini II, but soon after the arrival of the *Heavenbridge*, in a friendly competition with her colleagues, Keiko had successfully championed Onogoro as the planet's name.

So far, however, she had made her greatest contribution to the expedition with an extraordinary feat of applied linguistics—though she was bitterly aware that it was a feat with feet of clay.

After xenologist Andrik Norn and cyberneticist Betti Songa, accompanied by the floater pilot Farrell Sixkiller, had made contact with the Kybers and persuaded a solitary representative of their kind to return with them to the Onogoro Expeditionary Platform, Keiko had

taught that alien—whom Andrik had designated the
"septa-prime" of one of their innumerable "families
of seven"—first the rudiments and later the niceties of
Translic, the pan-global tongue spoken by all expedition members.

In the inflatable knowledge centre atop the Platform,
these tutoring sessions had taken place for nearly fifty
of the local days, for the Kyber was punctual in its
habit. It arrived at dawn every morning and ascended
via the elevator inside the Platform's central riser to the
knowledge centre; at sunset it descended by this same
conveyance to the mist- and stone-carpeted rubble
comprising the plains and amphitheatres of the
Onogorovan landscape. Between times, sweating like a
stevedore beneath her singlet, Keiko drilled the Kyber
in fundamentals and marvelled at its quickness. She
relished her work. Thrilled with each new breakthrough, she secretly prided herself on the fact that,
seemingly alone among her colleagues, she was making spectacular progress toward unlocking the mysteries of this world and its unlikely inhabitants. The
others were half in awe of her. But her success, she
knew, was primarily owing to the Kyber itself.

The creature learned rapidly. Keiko shared with it
Translic versions of Greek poetry, ancient Vedic literature, anthologies of haiku and other Oriental poetic
forms, Elizabethan and Restoration drama, Sufi teaching parables, scientific monographs, the lyrics of
popular songs from a dozen different cultures, and a
large amount of dust-dry technical manuals and
philosophical treatises, both ancient and modern. By
its fifth week of instruction the Kyber could communicate with expedition members as eloquently as any
word-drunk poet or university don, even to the point of
trotting out sophisticated double entendres and cun-

ningly apropos snippets of Japanese, English vulgate, and scholastic Latin. It absorbed and processed vocabularies as if its mind—its watch movements of concept and reason—were specifically geared to a universal grammar still more or less opaque to human understanding.

A grammar *literally* universal, Keiko often reminded herself; a grammar programmed into the very data of which the cosmos was composed.

Toward the end, in fact, Keiko had found herself regarding her alien disciple with a real sense of awe. The Kyber was her student saint, a messenger of the Hidden Ineffable, and that she should be its mentor rather than it hers went against a basic premise of the natural order. She spent more and more of her teaching time staring raptly at the Kyber and trying to fathom its thought processes. It *knew*, she felt, what humanity could only guess at . . .

Physically, the "septa-prime" who came to her for language lessions looked more like a Giacometti sculpture than a human being. Even when they sat face to face at the circular table in the knowledge centre, the alien towered over her. Although its torso seemed to be basically organic, invested with a papery sort of flesh reminiscent of a mummy's unravelling grave-cloths, its limbs glinted like new chrome and its head reared above its body like a mahogany mask backed by a big, carven halo. (It was the Kyber's circular crest, along with its metallic gleam, that belatedly reminded Keiko of the statues of Kannon in Sanjusangendo.) The creature's face was something turned on a lathe, only the mouth moving flexibly. When the Kyber spoke, Keiko half believed that its melodious, feminine voice issued from a recording unit concealed in the cavity behind its breast bone.

Finally, the eyes. They were a pair of horizontal hourglasses mounted in two rectangular patches with the appearance of wet sailcloth. Each eye had a binary pupil, as if the twin suns of the Gemini system, Dextro and Laevo, had dictated this startling physical adaptation to their varying light spectra. Keiko had no idea what to make of them.

Andrik, who went daily among the roofless Kyber palaces sunken like gigantic potholes at approximately kilometre intervals across the plain, argued that the two forward-facing pupils viewed the world stereoscopically, probably by Dextro light, while the peripheral bulbs functioned independently of each other, with a specific attunement to the radiation shed by Laevo. Also, the xenologist reported, he had observed that during a periodic Kyber ritual involving the "worship" of each family's septa-prime (an office that seemed to rotate like Pass the Parcel among the seven members of the countless, unforthcoming clans) their lateral pupils swelled furiously while the front-facing ones diminished to tiny points. What these optical responses meant, however, neither Andrik nor Betti Songa could say, and Keiko's student was no help because, despite its progress in Translic, it refused to answer direct inquiries about its people's origins, physiology, or social institutions.

"You haven't even told me your name," Keiko said one afternoon toward the close of a teaching session. "We've been doing this for—let's see—exactly forty-three of your planet's days. I've answered every one of your questions that I could and talked quite a lot about myself, but you've offered nothing in return. This is extremely frustrating! Why do you insist on holding yourself and your people at arm's length!"

"I insist on nothing," the creature said matter-of-factly.

"Tell me your name, then—your own private name."

"Why, Lady Keiko? One of your team members has given us the generic name Kybers, hasn't she? So you call us all. If I may ask, from what does this term derive?"

Keiko had never used the word *Kyber* in the presence of her imposing student, but she was not surprised that it had picked up on the term from Betti and the others. Nor was she surprised that it had met her question with a question of its own. Ever placid and serene, the alien nevertheless appeared to enjoy outwitting her probing tactics.

"Well," Keiko said, rising from her chair and walking to the enormous window-lens of the knowledge centre, too weary to evade the creature's trap, "*Kyber* is a derivation of *Kyborg*."

Outside, beyond the Platform's safety railings, was a vast panorama of canted stone walls and craterlike atria—the open "palaces" in which the aliens conducted their spartan, seemingly meaningless lives. For once, no rolling mists obscured the view.

"*Kyborg?*" the Kyber prompted her.

"That's Betti's own variation of *cyborg,* meaning a human being or an animal made over into a machine. But cyborg seemed too *soft* a name for your people to Betti."

"Why?"

Keiko turned and faced the alien. "Because the natives of Onogoro appear to have begun their lives as sentient robots, that later suffered a grotesque infestation of organic matter—flesh sprouting from chrome.

Kyborg struck Betti, I guess, as the right word, the right sound, to convey this impression of your people. The rest of us must have agreed, and so you became Ky-bers.''

Would putting the matter in just this way insult or discomfit the alien? Apparently not. It neither flinched from Keiko's gaze nor shed the aura of serenity radiating from the otherwise unreadable features.

"Betti is a cyberneticist," Keiko said, returning from the window and taking up her place opposite the Kyber. "I'm afraid that she regards you—all of you—as the self-perpetuating products of some sort of elaborate control system which no longer has any function or significance in the real world."

The Kyber, after fixing her with an uncomfortable lengthy stare, said, ''Could that not be a paraphrase of one of the popular definitions of the human species on your own planet?''

Taken aback, Keiko dropped her eyes. This rhetorical question was as close to a private revelation, at least in its implications, as the Kyber had ever permitted itself to utter. Looking up again, Keiko noticed that the alien was again exuding from the pin-hole pores along its arms a clear but vinegary-smelling sweat. Betti Songa claimed that this was a lubricant distilled from the limited variety of food-stuffs the Kybers ingested, but because their visitor was careful never to leave a sample of the substance smeared along a chair back or a table top, they had not been able to test this hypothesis. All Keiko knew was that occasionally the Kyber would begin to ''sweat'', filling the air with the tang of vinegar. Then, after a brief few moments, the process would cease and the smell eventually dissipate.

Andrik had once advanced the notion that Keiko's student, here in the knowledge centre, and the other

Kybers, yonder in their ruined amphitheatres, initiated the "sweating" process only in the presence of expedition members, as a form of mocking comment on human mortality. Or maybe (he had added offhandedly) the release of the substance and its attendant odours encoded a tactile and olfactory "language" specific to the machinelike Kybers. Keiko had ducked her head at this—for even if she weren't a chemist, Andrik's speculation bore directly on linguistic territory and spotlighted the vast areas of her own failure.

"You do not answer," the Kyber said.

Keiko started. "Oh," she managed, struggling to recall its question. "Perhaps you're right. I have never been an expert on definitions of the human species."

"Are you a hard one?" the Kyber asked.

"A hard one?" Keiko was at a loss. Non sequiturs were seldom part of her student's conversational arsenal.

"We are called Kybers because Betti Songa perceives us as hard. Your name similarly contains a double hardness—*kei, ko*—for which reason I assume that in spite of your anatomy you are actually one of us. A Kyber in your soul. Is that not likely, Lady Keiko?"

"You're teasing—no, you're *mocking* me." Keiko, whose hands were on the table top, dug her nails into her own palms.

The Kyber did not reply.

"Tell me your name," she urged the creature. "Tell me what you call your species, the word for your world, the secret names of your suns! How long have you been here? What do you hope for? How do you communicate with one another, if not through spoken language? How did you come to be? And why won't you respond even to the most harmless of direct enquiries?" She pounded both fists on the table, then averted her gaze. Her eyes stung, and she felt her heart stagger in her breast like a great scarlet butterfly in a high wind.

After a time the Kyber said, melodiously, "There is no inquiry whose answer does not contain a programme for evil, Lady Keiko."

"Or for good," she countered. "If you wish to bandy aphorisms."

"Or for good," the Kyber acknowledged placidly. "Inquire of me if I will be here for tomorrow's session."

Keiko's heart tore. Had she alienated her unpredictable alien past recovery? But, trying to calm herself, she obediently asked the Kyber if it intended to appear for another session.

"Of course," it responded. "Of course I so intend."

With that, the creature rose on the extensible stilts of its legs and strode with unwavering dignity to the door of the knowledge centre, more like an animate statue than a living organism. Briefly, Keiko wondered if its head was going to crash into the lintel, and almost shouted a warning. But at the last moment, without pausing in its stride, it telescoped just sufficiently to exit, and she watched it pass the window-lens on its way to the Platform's central riser.

The Kyber kept its word. It returned the following day, and the three days thereafter. Then abruptly—and totally without warning—it ceased to rendezvous with Keiko. Suspecting that she had naively played into the creature's hands, she began to reproach herself for her gullibility. Her failure, she felt, was as spectacular as had been the Kyber's ready success in absorbing the vocabularies and grammars of a half dozen human languages in addition to Translic. Her student's defection angered, humiliated, and saddened her.

Worse, Captain Hsi scrupulously refrained from
chastising her for her failure. Even Andrik—volatile
Andrik—sometimes had the air, when she cornered
him in the evenings and asked about his and Betti
Songa's progress with the aliens on the Onogorovan
plain, of one tiptoeing over a pie crust. This delicacy
with her Keiko took as an affront.

To make up for the Kyber's defection, Andrik and
Betti had spent every day of the last frigid week doing
"field work" in and around the labyrinthine crater
where they had first encountered the alien. Their hope
was to coax yet another Kyber from either that family or
a contiguous one to accompany them back to the
Platform aboard the expeditionary floater piloted by
Farrell Sixkiller. No such luck. In fact, not since their
initial success with Keiko's student had anyone but
Keiko been able to get through to a representative of the
aliens. Of late Andrik and Betti had found their in-the-
field options reduced to bemused observation and discreet anatomical measurements—for their presence in
the roofless atria of the various families was tolerated as
if they were either invisible or completely unworthy of
notice.

Now that Keiko's star student had dropped out of
school, the Kybers had virtually shut down all organic
function. When the xenologist, the cyberneticist, and
the floater pilot threaded their way through the inevitable maze-walls of a Kyber palace to its central chamber (Sixkiller blazing their way inward with the eerie
markings of a phosphor-pen), they found the aliens
frozen in a variety of perhaps emblematic postures.
Sight measurements and holophotography were possible in these circumstances, but any attempt to touch the
Kybers provoked brief defensive responses—the

swinging of an arm, the canting of a halo-crest—that were too dangerous to risk. As a consequence (Keiko soon came to realize) Andrik was slowly falling victim to the same sense of inadequacy and despair that continued to plague her.

THREE

In the refectory, on the afternoon of the day prior to her midnight deployment of the thousand golden images of Kannon, Keiko tried to goad her lover back into his usual talkativeness.

"Is there a causal relationship between the two events?" Keiko asked Andrik. "Did my Kyber desert me because it was time for a mass hibernation? Or is the mass hibernation a consequence of my being jilted by the Kyber?"

"Probably," Andrik said.

"Which then?" she demanded. He wasn't being playful; he was simply evading the issue. It was a retake of countless tête-à-têtes with the alien—except that Andrik had never in his life exuded serenity, even when fatigued or depressed.

"Kei," he said, setting aside his bowl of noodles and intercepting her gaze, "I can't possibly tell you. All I can say is that the two events *look* to be related, all right?"

He was not handsome. His eyes, set deep in his head, reminded Keiko of a pair of retort blisters full of thin, swirling smoke. Despite his exhaustion he smouldered.

"What's your *feeling*?" she insisted.

"His feeling is that the dead are alive, the living dead," interjected Farrell Sixkiller, who was sitting two tables away with Captain Hsi Ching-kuo and the novice planetologist Clemencia Venáges. "He'd rather be out there with the Kybers than up here with us fallible, decaying mortals."

"Shut up, Sixkiller." Andrik did not turn his head to address the floater pilot. With the understandable exception of Captain Hsi, Sixkiller was the only expedition member whom Andrik would not call by his given name.

Keiko glanced around. Everyone in the refectory— an inflatable structure twenty metres in diameter, with a hoop-girdered corridor to the galley and another to the research complex—had paused to take in the developing quarrel.

Immediately to Keiko's right sat the burly astrophysicist Craig Olivant, the computer officer Sharon Yablon, and the unflappable Betti Songa, her cinnamon-dark face strikingly highlighted by the fluorescents. At a trio of tables near the galley corridor were seven other expedition members; they included the floater pilot Milius, two Platform mechs, the chemist Heinrich Eshleman, the atmospheric specialist Nikolai Taras, the medic whose name Keiko could never get right, and the dowdy ecologist and molecular biologist Naomi Davis. Naomi, a friendly face, had taken Keiko under her wing at Luna Port several weeks before the departure of the *Heavenbridge* for the Gemini system.

None of these people was hypocritical enough to feign a lack of interest in the words exchanged by Sixkiller and Andrik. Involvement in others' affairs was unavoidable when you lived in your colleagues' pockets atop an expeditionary platform. In fact, Keiko noticed, the only person in the refectory who had continued to eat, wielding his chopsticks with deft indifference to the possibility of conflict, was Captain Hsi, who had just that afternoon returned from a mysterious sojourn of about fifteen hours aboard the *Heavenbridge*. His presence at table with Sixkiller suggested to Keiko that he and the floater pilot had resumed the intimacy that had evolved between them on the journey out from Luna Port.

"Andrik," she whispered, hoping to dissuade him from a display of temper in the captain's hearing.

"The refectory is a democratic place of assembly," Sixkiller declared loudly, looking around the room at the faces turned toward him. "Whatever your hoitytoity status when we're on duty, Dr Norn, you don't command me in here."

There was a chilly silence.

Keiko glanced at Captain Hsi. Why didn't he intervene? Sixkiller, despite the enforced democracy of their meal times, deserved a swift and certain rebuke.

Captain Hsi finished eating, then casually stood up. He was tall for a Chinese—taller than Andrik—with a concave face and protruding, heavy-lidded eyes. Only his close-cropped grey hair and snug-fitting military tunic undercut his resemblance to an emaciated Pekinese, thus preserving his dignity. He sorted his dinnerware, picked up his tray, and headed for the conveyor belt near the galley corridor. Here, all eyes upon him, he halted, put down his tray, and turned back toward the expectant gathering.

"I expect you to be civil to one another," he said mincingly. Then he singled out the astrophysicist at Betti Songa's table for instruction. "When you've finished here, Dr. Olivant, please join me in the observatory. We have work to do.'' Whereupon he pivoted, grabbed up his parka and mittens from the cloak shelf, and departed through the tunnel to the lab complex.

Keiko was appalled. Captain Hsi's leavetaking implied tacit approval of Sixkiller's baiting of Andrik—or if not approval, a stupid and unwarranted tolerance. So long as they didn't maim each other in a macho brawl, he appeared to be washing his hands of their conflict. Keiko did not entirely understand the captain's rationale for such behaviour, but she knew that he and Clemencia Venáges—insofar as Sixkiller was concerned—comprised what Andrik cynically called an ''unstable binary''. The floater pilot took turns revolving about one or the other of these people, who somehow managed to maintain their own relationship in a state of uneasy equilibrium. Keiko was not sure how the three of them made this arrangement work (if they did), but she had never before had cause to worry about the dynamics of the situation. Previously, she had based her estimation of Captain Hsi on the obvious efficiency of his command and her unspoken pride that he, too, was an Oriental.

''What do you think, Dr. Norn?'' Sixkiller piped up again. ''Is it possible for a machine to die? Contrariwise, of course, is it possible for a machine to live?''

''They're not machines,'' Andrik said deliberately.

Sixkiller gestured carelessly at Betti Songa. ''Then why do we send a cyberneticist out to study them, too?''

''Don't you three ever talk when you're in the field together?'' Keiko asked. ''Why this hostility, Farrell?

And why vent it in front of people who have other matters to discuss?''

"Outside," he responded, "I keep my mouth shut, and I do my job."

"But not in here? Why not? What tomahawk are you grinding today?"

Betti Songa interrupted, her tongue like a pink petal in a deep-umber bowl: "He believes the Kybers were created by an extra-Geminid species to exterminate the original inhabitants and then to colonize the planet for their absentee masters. Being one thirty-second native American, he sympathizes with the extinct natives—whatever, whoever, they might have been—and deplores our fawning attention to the Kybers, their murderers."

"That's absurd," remarked Craig Olivant.

Before Sixkiller could protest, Betti added, "We send both a xenologist and a cyberneticist to study the Kybers because they're so obviously something new under the suns, at least to us. A conjoining of the organic with the mechanical, not through engineering but through a natural cybergenetic process. Just because we have no precedent for that process back home doesn't mean it can't exist elsewhere, Farrell. It's a big cosmos."

"They're *made* creatures," Sixkiller insisted. "Anyone can see that. And they probably didn't originate here, either."

"That's absolute nonsense," said Naomi Davis from across the refectory. She was a Britisher, usually as plain-spoken and down-to-the-sod as a farmer, despite her years and her education. "Andrik has told us that they harvest those great stonelike succulents out there, hasn't he? Those *lithops*-like things. And they cull all sorts of pesky vermin from the crannies of their labyrinths. Machines don't eat, at least not organic matter. The Kybers would have *had* to evolve here— here in this system, Farrell—to do so well on such unlikely local fare. Not to mention the fact that every species of wild life we've encountered to date has the same binary eye structure. Those beasties aren't gyroscopic toys somebody's revved up and set loose here, either.''

''What makes you so sure?'' Sixkiller challenged her.

Keiko glanced at Andrik. He was eating again, spooning noodles into his mouth and following the others' debate with merry eyes. Through no doing of his own he was becalmed in the eye of the storm. Grinning, he offered Keiko a portion of his bean-curd entrée. She shook her head, ran a concerned finger along his wrist.

''Very well,'' Naomi Davis was saying. ''Let's suppose the Kybers have drastically modified their natural evolution. Let's suppose they've rebuilt themselves. They still must share with the rest of Onogoro's biota an organic archeohistory going back hundreds of millions of years. Even the form of their rebuilding—if you really want to call it that—is probably inspired by the adaptive morphology of the local wild life.''

''Adaptive morphology?'' Sixkiller echoed her.

''Certainly. You know those rubbery tortoise-things that are just now hardening off among the *lithops*. You've seen them. And what about the big, mottled 'snailies' secreting their ceramic shells? The Kybers' rigid exoskeletons may seem several steps above these examples in complexity, I grant you—but I'm still convinced that our aliens once wore quasi-human skins that periodically hardened into a kind of protective armour. Working from the natural processes of the Onogorovan mock-tortoises and snailies, they may have painstakingly redesigned themselves."

"Why?" asked Clemencia Venáges, deflecting from Sixkiller a degree of the others' civilized fury. "To adapt to the cycles of freeze and thaw here on Onogoro?"

"It's a possibility," replied the ecologist.

"Only if they evolved here," Sixkiller said. "And they didn't. They're incapable of evolution." His wounded doe's eyes bleeding entreaty, he nodded at Olivant. "Tell them, sir. Tell 'em why it's unlikely anything on Onogoro evolved here."

Olivant, a mane of blond hair clasped in a metal barrette at his nape, pushed his tray aside. "At the moment, Farrell, I can't make *any* sort of authoritative pronouncement about life on this world. I've been too busy stargazing."

"That's a hedge. Tell 'em what we've recently discovered."

Keiko looked at the floater pilot as did Andrik and the others. He was using "we've" in a ridiculously proprietorial manner, even if he had recently been privy to some important confidential information. By no stretch of the imagination was he a scientist.

"Tell them," Sixkiller urged, "that we've goofed, that we've jumped to a false conclusion. Namely, that this planet is habitable simply because its inhabited."

"You're speaking in riddles," Keiko said, exasperated. Turning her head to find Andrik comically shushing her, she realized that she had just drawn Sixkiller's gaze back to their table.

"Even so, he's correct about Onogoro," Craig Olivant conceded, rescuing them again. The astrophysicist proceeded to sketch great, boomeranging ellipses in the air with his bearlike right arm; the ellipses gyrated overhead around an imaginary sun.

"This orbit around Dextro-Gemini isn't stable," Craig told the group. "That means our planet can't have been in orbit longer than a few thousand years, if that. It's been captured. And, as Farrell has been rather smugly hinting, it's going to be uncaptured again."

Andrik's wrist jumped under Keiko's hand. "When?" he asked.

"Soon," Craig said, "speaking in terms of standard months. Probably when Onogoro is approximately equidistant between Dextro and Laevo— an event that will occur on this very revolution."

Sixkiller put in, hurriedly, "And a planet that's only been in orbit around its primary a few thousand years just isn't going to support the kind of continuous evolution leading to the Kybers."

"There go your original victims of genocide, too," Betti Songa pointed out. "What do you *really* have against the Kybers, Farrell?"

"That they're machines," he replied readily enough. "That they're dead things mimicking the essence of life and making us believe in their clumsy masquerade. Somebody or something sinister put them here."

"Right now," Keiko said, a sad guilt descending upon her like a shroud, "they're not even *mimicking* life."

Andrik turned his chair so that he was facing Craig Olivant. A tic at the corner of the xenologist's mouth betrayed his excitement.

"Maybe their lack of animation is preparation for the inevitable decoupling," he said, an unthinking sop to Keiko's conscience. "They were pretty quiescent when we arrived, back at the end of 'summer' when the temperature must have topped all of twelve Centigrade. The colder it got, though, the more animated they became. It was almost as if they were reacting to our presence, unthawing as we fed the example of life into their environment. I had actually begun to think the cold was *stimulating* them.''

"Me, too," Betti said. "Until Keiko's student began playing hooky and they all clocked back down again."

"Exactly," Sixkiller interjected. " 'Clocked back down'—like wind-up mechanisms running at someone else's bidding."

Andrik ignored this. "Craig, now that we're swinging out toward Laevo, what's going to happen?"

The astrophysicist raised his thick, blond eyebrows and smiled apologetically. Shaking his head, he gathered his dinnerware together. "Is everyone finished eating?" he asked, standing.

"Why?" Andrik asked in turn.

"Because if you are, I'll take all interested parties outside to illustrate our situation with a visual aid."

FOUR

Bundled in heat-recycling parkas, five people left the refectory and strolled across the gleaming deck plates of the Platform to its western railing: Craig, Betti, Andrik, Sixkiller, and Keiko. Surprisingly, it was still twilight, the sky a disquieting mauve and the plain afire with vermilion scintillations. The cold bit at Keiko's lips, reached down into her lungs.

There—over to the northwest—Dextro was a trembling tangerine sinking behind the line of broken mountains beyond the plain. The fog on the icy marshes east of the mountains flickered with quicksilver glints, and the wind hooting over the lips of the sunken Kyber atria sounded in her ears like discordant oboe music. Twilight always astonished Keiko. Every dreadnought of mist, every rounded gnarl of lithoid vegetation, every inhabited crater partook of the same bleak but beautiful strangeness. Although still not acclimatized to the forbidding peculiarities of Onogoro, in some ways she was happy that her candid wonder persisted.

"Look there," Craig said, jabbing a fat thermal mitten at the sky.

Andrik exhaled a long plume of vapour. "That's just Il Penseroso, isn't it? Nothing unusual there."

Il Penseroso was Dextro's massive inner planet, a rock ball twice the diameter of Earth and ten times its density. Onogoro had no natural satellite, but Il Penseroso showed the party on the Platform a twilit disc, as if it were indeed a sort of distant, poor-relation moon. Keiko thought the planet an eerie, breathtaking apparition.

"Hell," said Craig, "that's my visual aid. I'm fairly sure that our last conjunction with the inner planet had decoupled Onogoro's weird ellipse around Dextro. The Kybers are going to fly off into deep space aboard a runaway planet. Us, too, if we remain."

In the aching twilight everyone studied the sky.

"We can easily save ourselves," Keiko finally announced, her teeth like icicle nubs against her tongue and lips. "But what about the Kybers? Can they survive being hurled into the void?"

"Survive?" hooted Sixkiller. "Survival isn't an innate attribute of machines. Persistence maybe, but not survival. Besides, they're already dead."

"Perhaps they can," Craig told her, as if the floater pilot had never spoken. Then, like a priest of infinity, he sketched in midair a looping figure eight.

"Their salvation may be this: Onogoro is exchanged between the two suns every few thousand years. To the heavy inner planet circling Dextro, you see, corresponds another such world circling Laevo. Il Penseroso over here, good ole El Pesado over there. Our assumption is that the lighter elements created during the origins of this system were all blown clear by the radiation pressures of the two suns. The result was two fat-boy inner planets and our own lovely, lonely Onogoro. Computer simulations in our observatory here and also upstairs aboard the *Heavenbridge* verify the workability of an alternating orbit for the Kybers' world. Given these conditions, folks, you can have a permanently unstable orbit.''

Keiko could feel her cold-numbed lips forming a smile. ''The Kybers have adapted to periodic switchovers, then.''

''The air will freeze,'' Sixkiller objected. ''Say your hypotheses about these alternating orbits and the aliens as living beings do happen to be correct. It's still not likely that *things* as complex as the Kybers could evolve on a world that keeps passing back and forth between two suns, is it? What about the different intensities of radiation, the different sorts of climatic conditions that would result on Onogoro?'' Even inside his plush-lined hood, the man's face was offended and disbelieving.

''How the hell could Craig possibly know for sure?'' Andrik rejoined, tapping the floater pilot on the chest. ''Are those possibilities less acceptable to you than the idea that Great Sinister Somethings put the Kybers down here to seduce humanity into sin? We're not devotees of God the Machine, Sixkiller. We haven't yet elevated the Kybers to Golden Calf status.''

''If the alternating-orbit hypothesis *is* correct,'' Craig quickly put in, ''all I can hazard about the atmosphere is that it probably won't freeze. The planet's going to pick up heat from Laevo as it leaves Dextro behind. Winter's going to get a whole helluva lot more wintery before the first spring thaw, sure—but that thaw's gonna come, folks, it's definitely gonna come.'' The big man hunched his shoulders and nodded at the vibrant, falling sun. ''Provided Dextro doesn't . . .''

''Doesn't what?'' Sixkiller prodded him.

''Captain Hsi wants to talk to me,'' Craig said. ''He's waiting in the observatory, and I'm late.''

"I'll go with you," Sixkiller declared.

"The hell you will!" Vapour curling draconically from the corners of his mouth, Craig glowered at the other man. "You'll stay out of the observatory until or unless you're invited to enter."

Keiko heard herself chuckling nervously. In his sudden explosive wrath the astrophysicist had become even more imposing than usual. The floater pilot, abashed, blinked at Craig, then clasped the railing with his mittens and stared lugubriously toward Dextro.

"I'm late," Craig repeated, as if apologizing. "It's just that we may have to abandon Onogoro during transit between its decoupling from the Dextro orbit and its recapture by Laevo. These petty arguments about the nature of the Kybers will necessarily give way to close observation of the gravitational mechanics of the switchover, probably from aboard the *Heavenbridge*." He paused again, then concluded: "If we're permitted to stick around this system at all."

"Why wouldn't we be?" Betti asked.

"That's what I'm not able to divulge just yet," Craig replied. "I'm not trying to be unduly mysterious, either. You'll learn soon enough—maybe even by tomorrow, folks." He hunched his shoulders, nodded a curt farewell, and turned to lumber away toward the Platform's lab complex and observatory.

"Wait a minute!" Andrik shouted after him. "How long is this transit between Dextro and Laevo going to take?"

Craig looked back toward them, the plush of his hood half obscuring his meaty face. "Using the former orbit around Dextro as a standard, Onogoro's going to be sailing through no-man's-land, the Dread In-Between Sea, for one and a third local years. That's a little more than two E-years, Andrik." He waved, resumed his trek toward the observatory.

"You mean we're going to have to abandon our study of the Kybers for two goddamn years?" Andrik shouted.

Craig, still walking, did not even look back. "Unless you're willing to sit out the winter transit on this Platform," he called. "Or unless you can entice a couple of Kybers aboard the *Heavenbridge*."

Andrik put an arm around Keiko's waist and pulled her to him. The contact was so muffled that she felt grappled at rather than caressed. "Not bloody likely," he muttered.

"Hallelujah," said Sixkiller quietly.

Releasing Keiko, Andrik whirled on the man. "Ignorance spawns hatred, Sixkiller. In turn, hatred of the Kybers—if it prevails as an official attitude—is going to contribute to our *remaining* ignorant about them. How the hell can you justify this know-nothing, no-win quackery? How the hell can you justify it even to yourself?"

Sixkiller smiled, his eyes dancing. "See no evil, hear no evil—"

"Speak no evil," Andrik concluded in disgust, shaking his head. "You're as phony as a plastic peace pipe."

"Or as a 'life form' made out of bauxite and redwood, hey?"

Keiko grasped Andrik's upper arm with both hands, gently. "You sound like children, snotty-faced little boys. It's cold out here, getting colder. I suggest that you both return to your dormicles."

"I'll take this one to safety," Betti said, pushing Sixkiller away from the railing. "Anyway, he and I have a board game to finish in the common room.''

"I may be wanted elsewhere," said Sixkiller evasively.

"Then you'd certainly better get there, hadn't you?''
Like a collie outflanking a truculent pup, Betti herded
the floater pilot toward the recreation inflatable near the
dormitories.

When Betti and Sixkiller had disappeared into the
deepening umber shadows Andrik said, ''What a lout.
Even if he's had no scientific training, he's not an
uneducated man. There's no excuse.''

"He's afraid of the Kybers," Keiko said.

"Then he's a coward as well as a lout.''

Vaguely disappointed, Keiko shook her head. "His
fear isn't merely a private faint-heartedness. You know
him to be courageous in the performance of his duties.
It's an abstract sort of fear on the behalf of all of us.
He's afraid for humanity, Andrik.''

"He sees us all as Indians before the fateful coming
of the White Man." The xenologist laughed sardonically.

"Perhaps he does.''

"Well, Kei, his abstract fear is a cliché, and like
most fears it stems from ignorance.''

"Perhaps it does.''

"And now it seems that even celestial mechanics are
conspiring to put a holy imprimatur on the ignorance he
worships.''

"That's not Sixkiller's fault.''

"I know." Andrik released a heavy, cloudy breath,
deliberately calming himself. ''It still makes me angry.''

They talked a little longer, and Keiko invited Andrik
to spend the night in her dormicle. They had not slept
together since the defection of her alien student, six

local days ago. Since then, Andrik's "chivalrous" refusal to discuss her failure had scarcely had the amicable effects of an aphrodisiac. Further, Andrik had been returning to the Platform these last several evenings morose and care-worn. The moratorium on their love-making had developed by unspoken mutual consent. This evening marked the first occasion in days that she had felt the need for both intimate conversation and physical closeness. Besides, the mass hibernation of the Kybers might be owing to the impending decoupling of Onogoro from Dextro rather than from any sin of commission or omission during her tutoring of the septa-prime. Now her lover appeared ready to discuss recent events, and she was ready to join her flesh with Andrik's. Smiling faintly, the xenologist accepted her invitation.

"Is it too early to sack out now?" he asked her.

"Yes," she said, returning his smile. "You go back to the complex, get your things. I want to finish watching Dextro set. I'll meet you in my dormicle, well, what about two hours from now?"

"All right."

After some bantering small talk, Andrik put his nose to hers, Eskimo fashion, then trotted back across the rime-coated deck plates to the warmth of the living facilities.

Keiko, comfortable in her thermals despite the biting cold, watched Dextro sink behind the mountains. A flat orange glow spread across their jagged crests, then spilled down their flanks toward the lakes of fog hovering over the marshes east of the foothills. Beautiful— but the magic was surreal, an act of systematic delirium, as if an invisible hand had squeezed icy juice from the tangerine sun and then basted the mountains with it. The crater dwellings on the plain also got a quick swipe with that brush, and Keiko imagined that a few wakeful Kybers were staring up at the lamp-lit Platform even as she stared down across the twilight desolation of their world. What was she—what were any of her colleagues—doing here?

A hand fell across Keiko's shoulder.

She started, swung about, and found herself confronting a wide-eyed Farrell Sixkiller, his irises marbled with the colours of sunset.

"Dr Norn has one very basic and crippling hang-up," the floater pilot informed her, not quite whispering.

Keiko instinctively retreated a step.

"I've been with him in the Kyber palaces, you know. He believes the aliens to be a genuine life form."

"So does Betti, even if she is a cyberneticist. So do I, for that matter. I taught one to speak Translic, after all."

"No, no, you don't understand, Dr Takahashi, Dr Norn also believes that they embody an answer— maybe *the* answer—to the riddle of the cosmos."

Keiko laughed.

"I mean it. He thinks them the key to the very meaning of our existence."

Certain that the man was touched with a peculiarly virulent form of 'decoupling madness', Keiko stared at Sixkiller.

"It's true," he declared.

"You're distorting the nature of his involvement, Farrell, mistaking the depth of his commitment for— for I don't know what."

"He's obsessed with what I told you."

"So are you, it seems."

"I don't like seeing anyone search after ultimate

meaning in places where there's no blood, no gyzym, no juice. The Kybers are machines—very advanced machines, maybe, but still machines. Whatever sacrificed its birthright to engineer them has paid the price of extinction for its vanity. Dr Norn refused to recognize that fact. He thinks the Kybers will be able to tell him who coded the acorn.''

Keiko felt that, mutedly, Sixkiller was raving; none of what he said made any straightforward sense. ''You're a pantheist,'' she said, testing the description mentally. ''You're a Shintoist in eagle feathers.''

''Without the goddamn feathers. I see no spirit in these death-worshipping mechanical aliens—except an evil one. Machines have no souls, Dr Takahashi.''

''This from a floater pilot? From a man who has many times entrusted his life to the mercy of the *Heavenbridge?*''

''Controllable machines, Dr Takahashi.''

''Whereas the Kybers—''

''Are machines that seek to control the organic processes and the organic beings that you and I represent. Therefore, they're our enemies. If he thinks them good fodder for xenological study, Dr Norn is a traitor to life. Meanwhile, Dr Takahashi, the Kybers are agents of entropy and death.''

''Farrell—'' She hoped that the reptition of his first name might soften him enough to employ hers.

''Now they lie in what Betti calls *kybertrance,*'' he interrupted her, ''a state almost indistinguishable from death, and their planet will soon be dragged off its Dextro orbit into the chill of winter transit.''

''Toward another sun,'' Keiko cautiously pointed out.

''Don't allow Dr Norn to come to you tonight. The Kybers have infected him with their own negative essence, Dr Takahashi. He's gradually taking on the deathly attributes of the machines he regards as oracles.''

Sixkiller was insane. Onogoro had undone him. To suppose Andrik surrendering to any sort of pernicious antilife force was to misread the character of the man. Keiko retreated another step. Although several centimetres shorter than Craig Olivant, Sixkiller was taller than Andrik, muscular in a sleek, catlike way, and only slightly less intense in his movements and enthusiasms. It was frightening to face him alone on the deserted outer margin of the expeditionary Platform. Nor did the anguished notes of a recorded synthesizer composition floating out to them from one of the inflatables have any power to allay Keiko's fear. The music seemed to isolate her even further.

''Since you're giving advice,'' she said, struggling to suppress both her anger and her fear, ''what would you have me do?''

Sixkiller seemed not to hear the question. ''Dr Norn is going to hurt you,'' he said. ''But he's going to hurt all of us if he continues to pursue this obsession of his.''

''And I shouldn't allow him to visit my dormicle?''

''Come to mine,'' Sixkiller said, smiling more gently than Keiko had ever seen him smile. ''Come to mine.''

''You've already formed alliances,'' Keiko told him. ''And I feel no physical attraction for you.''

''Captain Hsi? He hasn't time to think of such things lately, Keiko.'' (*There,* he had finally used her given name—but in a context that made her wish for a return to impersonal formality.) ''Besides, at present I'm in thrall to no one. Speaking solely of my private relationships, that is.''

Yes, thought Keiko, and you apparently regard me as

a warm but distant star to be wooed during winter transit. If so, you're wrong to interpret my willingness to hear you out as either desire or sympathy. . . .

Sixkiller, cocking his head attentively, seemed to read these thoughts in her face. "Good night, Dr Takahashi," he said quietly. He plunged his mittened hands into the pouch on the belly of his parka, then stalked back toward the common room and the melancholy basso sighing of the synthesizer. Keiko closed her eyes on his retreating figure.

FIVE

"Dear God, Kei, what's that?"

Andrik, a heat-quilt twisted about his legs, had just pulled himself to a sitting position on her bedstead. He was staring into the dormicle's holoniche at the nimbused and multiarmed statues of Kannon projected there from a microdot on a plastic card. Keiko wiped her eyes and looked at the xenologist. She saw him through a blur of tears and the lingering gold radiance shed by the images of the bodhisattva. Her dormicle had become the Hall of Mercy, and her lover had revived to its transfiguration.

"Sanjusangendo," she whispered.

"What?"

As best she could, Keiko explained. After their bout of love-making it had struck her that the Kybers of Onogoro bore a strong resemblance to the statues of Kannon in the Hall of Mercy. She did not tell Andrik that she had briefly seen his own body as a machine, nor that that perception had led her to make a startling connection between the benighted natives of this world

43

and the thousand enlightened Buddhas-to-be in the temple in Kyoto. If Kannon was holy, then a Kyber might also be holy. And if Andrik had briefly seemed a mindless mechanism rather than a living organism, well, perhaps his passion to understand could enlighten and transfigure him, too. Sixkiller's fear need not infect her and the others.

Everything was holy, rightly perceived.

"The resemblance is superficial," Andrik declared, studying the images in the holoniche. The figures in the foreground stood about a hand high; those behind them diminished in size until the faces on the tenth row were mere thumbnail masks coated with antique-gold polish. "Despite all those arms, Kannon has a human face."

Keiko said nothing.

"Can you imagine a host of Kybers standing in rows in a Buddhist temple, switched off—emblems of our human mercy if we decide to rescue them from this decoupling? Can you, Kei?"

"That's not going to happen."

"They worship one another, or did before they all shut down. Why shouldn't we join in?"

"Farrell Sixkiller says you've already begun." Keiko realized that, without meaning to, she had framed a kind of accusation.

"*He* worships ignorance. The Kybers my gods, and blissful ostrich ignorance his—that's the score, eh?"

Again Keiko held her tongue.

Andrik softened toward her, vowed that his remark about placing the Kybers in a Buddhist temple had been intended facetiously—as if she had not understood that much for herself. Noticing her pique, reading the depth of her melancholy, he grew jauntily philosophical:

"Sometimes, Kei, I think we've flown to the stars for one reason and one reason only: to worship at the shrine of the Strange. Having left our own shrines vacant, of course."

Now she spoke up: "That's too easy an anlaysis, Andrik. Besides, it's not true of Nippon. The shrines and temples *aren't* vacant there." It hurt to be separated from her country, and the trembling hologram of the statues of Kannon cruelly reinforced her sense of estrangement and loss.

"Is there a difference?" Andrik asked. "Between shrines and temples. I mean?"

"Temples are Buddhist, shrines are Shinto. Buddhism is the spiritual, meditative religion. Shinto is a celebration of the earth, of the flesh. But one doesn't choose between being a Buddhist or a Shintoist, Andrik. One is finally both. *Either,* in fact—from moment to moment, from day to day. As I am, even here on Onogoro."

"And the Kybers?"

"Having 'taught' one," she said laughing wanly, "I can easily imagine that an ultraintelligent biomachine might become a Buddhist. Such an entity represents pure thought, Andrik, thought beyond thought. But— like Sixkiller, I'm afraid—I don't know how such a creature could ever be a Shintoist. No flesh. No earth."

"A little sand, though," Andrik offered playfully. "Silicon circuitry, my Lady Kei."

She shook her head. "Sand gardens—rock gardens—are reflections of Buddhist reverie. As at Ryoanji Temple. Before I left my country for Luna Port, Andrik, I spent three hours sitting in the temple grounds contemplating that little sea of white sand with its fifteen stone islands. Then, the very next day, I joined the surge of millions up the hill above the Inari Shrine at Fushima—up through ten thousand vermilion torii gateways stationed shoulder to shoulder like . . .

like giant croquet wickets.'' She smiled, proud of this transnational analogy. ''And I? I was a corpuscle in the human bloodstream there, body pressing against body all the way to the top, gladly losing myself in the press.''

''So you're a Shintoist when you make love?''

Keiko flinched, then hoped that Andrik had not taken note. ''Perhaps.'' She turned off the projector; the statues of Kannon vanished. ''Viewed in that way, though, you should perhaps regard orgasm as Buddhist, a moment of nirvana.''

''Maybe this mass hibernation of the Kybers is a protracted communal orgasm, then. A time of enlightened cyber-thoughts. Kyber-thoughts. Or maybe it's a long Shinto memorial service, when they remembered what they were.''

''Sixkiller says they're dead.''

''But they can resurrect themselves to our idea of life, Kei. Maybe they live *through death*—just as we rejuvenate ourselves with sleep, taking the elevator of Morpheus down through the non-REM levels of consciousness to the REM floors of dreams. Their sleep is literally death, and their dreams are profound but inaccessible kyberthoughts.''

''Sleep doesn't rejuvenate you, Andrik. You fight it, waking up as hyper as you went to bed.''

Naked and trembling, Andrik cast aside the heat-quilt and donned a robe. A moment later he was pacing. He halted in front of the holoniche. ''Turn the projector back on, Kei.''

She did, and upon Andrik were superimposed, or interthreaded, the gleaming illusory images of the statues. He stepped aside, permitting the entire miniature scene to leap backward into the holoniche.

"There *is* more than a superficial resemblance," he said. "Kannon is inscrutable, and so are the Kybers. Their thoughts are beyond our apprehension— kyberthoughts, nirvana-thoughts."

"Then Sixkiller is right, Andrik: We'll never be able to comprehend them, at least not in this life."

Andrik resumed pacing, disrupting the hologram each time he passed in front of the projector. "Overloaded with data, they shut down," he said in a speculative tone. "They sleep—they *die*, rather—in order to process this data. They passed into stasis, into voluntary death, into genuine death—with the possibility of either a willed or an externally triggered resurrection. The mechanism for this awakening operates like a thermostat, switching them on again! They rejuvenate themselves through death!"

"You mean a cryostat, don't you?"

"Yes," Andrik said halting and pointing an appreciative finger at her. "Exactly. A cryostat." Then paced again. "What must they imagine when they're dead? That they're alive? And, when they've switched back on again, that they're . . . dead? That their awakening has plunged them back into the illusion and heartbreak of mere existence?"

Listening to Andrik's feverish self-interrogation, Keiko grew uneasy. The Kybers had infected him with their "negative essence," Sixkiller had said, and now, indeed, it seemed that there was something cold and entropic about her lover's obsession with them.

"What if we could kidnap a Kyber and chill it down to the temperature of liquid nitrogen in a cryotank?" he was asking. "Would its brain achieve light-speed reasoning? Would it pump its frozen limbs too fast for us to follow?"

"Andrik—"

"Death and cold are their natural mediums," he continued.

"Media," she corrected him half-heartedly. Just at the moment a touch of linguistic certitude felt like a port in a storm.

But he turned to address her directly. "Maybe I mean mediums as in seance? Their lateral pupils, Kei—their lateral pupils are their death-eyes. *Thanatoscopes*, call them. Instruments for perceiving life-in-death and death-in-life. It's certainly clear to me that they can see things beyond our ken, things out of our range of empirical and metaphysical perception."

"Hush," Keiko whispered.

"It's clear to me, too, that—"

"Hush," Keiko said, with tender emphasis.

Andrik's eyes widened and his lips remained parted. He was standing in a shimmer of tiny statues, his navy-blue robe and his pale flesh patterned with the golden overlay. He seemed stunned by her command.

"I love you, Andrik."

She repeated the words to herself, translating them for the first time mentally into Japanese—*kimi wo aishite iru*—acknowledging their boldness in her own language. For a man to say such a thing would be, well, affected. For a woman, it would almost be lacking in the sensitivity essential to love. Was this why, even though they had been physically involved with each other since their sixth week aboard the *Heavenbridge*, she had never said these words to him? Ah, no, it was different. They had been lovers, yes, but not each other's "loved ones." The distinction was not something that Keiko had ever understood very well, but Andrik, who had apparently survived two unsatisfactory formal alliances in his past, seemed to think it a meaningful and important one. Therefore, herself wary of possessing and being possessed, and remembering even in their Translic pillow talk her own dialect of love, Keiko had doubly honoured the xenologist's outspoken prescriptions against voicing a commitment deeper than occasional friendly access to each other's sympathy and person. Love for Andrik, she knew, was an unobtainable abstract akin to, well, to the secret knowledge of the Kybers. Now, however, Andrik had begun to believe that given half a chance he could grasp the hidden kernel of that knowledge and utterly encompass it. If that were so, as unhealthy as his preoccupation with the aliens loomed, then why could he not also comprehend the strictures and the liberations of another human being's love?

"Say again."

She repeated the words.

And he surprised her by saying, easily, and apparently with sincerity. "And I love you." He stepped toward her. The bodhisattvas shifted on his face. He looked like a picture puzzle of some kind of fragmented or endlessly replicated saint. Yes, that was it, thought Keiko, both amused and astonished: Andrik had been Kannonized. Saint or no, he nodded at the bed.

"Not just yet," she said, remembering her earlier image of him and the fears it had set galloping.

"Then let me hold you," he suggested. "It's cold, and I simply want to hold you, Kei."

So they lay together on Keiko's spartan bedstead, the heat-quilt crumpled atop them and their arms mercifully interlocked beneath its folds. They lay this way, her lips to his forehead, until Onogoro's dawn. The thousand illusory statues of Kannon kept watch.

SIX

A sound of faint chimes awakened Keiko. She arose, donned her abbreviated kimono, and went to the door. The monitor screen above it showed her Betti Songa, already dressed and alert, standing in the corridor.

"I'm here, Betti. What is it?"

The African woman spoke into the microphone in the dormicle's outside wall. "Captain Hsi wants all scientific personnel to gather at once in the observatory."

"Before breakfast?"

Betti laughed. "If you haven't already eaten, yes. You slugabed." She was gone.

Andrik was off the bed and nearly into his clothes before Keiko could relay this message, and a moment later they were on their way together through one of the Platform's hoop-girdered tunnels to the lab complex. The window-lenses in the corridor were completely frosted over with jumbled patterns of rime.

"Did it sleet last night?" Keiko asked Andrik.

He glanced at the ghost symbols on the window they were passing. "Only an Eskimo would know what to

call last night's weather. I rub noses, but I don't savvy
the one billion distinctions among different kinds of
snow. Thank Dextro, it looks clear again.'' Refracted
brilliance dazzled their eyes, as light shone through the
frost.

Assembled in the lecture room of the two-story observatory were most of Keiko's professional colleagues, less
than a dozen people. Four expedition members
were on a protracted floater trip over the southern
extremity of the Kyber continent; they had been gone
nearly eight local days. Because neither the Platform
mechs nor the floater pilots had been summoned to the
lecture room, Farrell Sixkiller was blessedly absent.

Squeezing past Sharon Yablon into the third row of
chairs horseshoeing the speaker's dais, Keiko was conscious not only of the lateness of her and Andrik's
entrance but of the nervous expectancy of the entire
group. Her own fear was that Captain Hsi was going to
announce an immediate abandonment of Onogoro because of its imminent decoupling from Dextro. Andrik
would not take that very well, she knew—nor did the
prospect of monitoring from the *Heavenbridge* the
planet's extraorbital pilgrimage toward Laevo particularly appeal to her, either. The transit would take almost
two standard years, and she would have next to nothing
to do. Surely they had another fifty or sixty local days in
which to make genetic analysis of Onogoro's strange
biota and to spy on the hibernating Kybers.

Surely . . .

Captain Hsi and Craig Olivant were standing together at a makeshift music-stand lectern, but Craig,
deferentially, had positioned himself a step or two
behind the captain.

''Ladies, gentleman,'' Captain Hsi began, speaking

Translic with no hesitancy and scarcely any accent this morning, ''Dr Olivant tells me that many of you are already aware that Dextro-Gemini II may soon legally change its name to *Laevo*-Gemini II.''

Hearty laughter greeted the captain's words. It sounded nervous and overquick to Keiko's ear, as if her colleagues were grasping at the slender reassurance of humour. Olivant smiled wanly, and Andrik, sitting on her right, stared fixedly at the captain without any change of expression, which was coolly neutral. The captain was not known for humour, even in situations that might warrant its use.

''No matter,'' Captain Hsi continued. ''If we pursue the planet with the *Heavenbridge*, we may yet call it with some accuracy,'' nodding meaningfully at Keiko, ''Onogoro.''

Much gentler laughter this time, and a smattering of polite applause as people, recalling the origin of this name in the Japanese creation myth, looked over their shoulders at Keiko and Andrik.

''Onokoro,'' strictly, but the tongues of the expedition hadn't quite fitted round the hardness of the syllable, so it had been softened by general consent. This was the name for the first ''naturally coagulated'' island—as it translated out—which was stirred in the primal waters by the demiurges Izanami and Izanagi as they stood on the Ama no Hasidate, Heaven's Bridge. For the first time Keiko shuddered at the name she had favoured. Had the Kybers coagulated naturally out of primal protoplasm? What lance had stirred them? Whose hand had held it?

''Some of you, I understand, do not happily anticipate renewed confinement aboard the *Heavenbridge* for the duration of such a mission.''

''He's read my mind,'' whispered Andrik sidelong.

"Mine, too," Keiko acknowledged. "Shhhh."

"In which case Dr Olivant and I may have a somewhat ambivalent kind of happy news for you." Captain Hsi stepped aside for the astrophysicist. "Dr Olivant, please."

Craig's long blond hair hung loose today. When he grasped the edges of the wobbly lectern, the stand slipped away from him. After catching and setting it right, Craig put his hands behind his back and pointed his chin toward his audience in a touchingly vulnerable way. He looked like a young Father Christmas, beardless and ruddy.

"The ambivalent happy news that Captain Hsi is talking about is just this," Craig said. "Dextro is showing warning signs of going nova. Since shortly after our research/reconnaissance team settled in on the Platform, Dr Mahindra and I have been working on this problem, and we're reasonably certain of our conclusions."

V. K. Mahindra, Keiko knew, was Craig's counterpart aboard the light-skimmer. Both the Platform and the ship were equipped with a full range of spectroscopic and heat measuring equipment, not to mention telescopes of the radio as well as the visible-light variety. Further, the *Heavenbridge* had dispatched a small remote probe toward Dextro and another towards Laevo within days of their arrival in the Gemini system.

No one moved, no one laughed, and Keiko could not discover even an ambivalent form of "happiness" in Craig's news.

"How soon?" asked Nikolai Taras, the atmospheric specialist.

"That's hard to tell," Craig replied. "No one has ever perched smack dab on top of a potential nova before, waiting for it to hatch."

"Give us an estimate," said Naomi Davis from the front row.

"Maybe six standard months from now, Naomi. Maybe five years. I suppose I should emphasize that we're in no immediate danger ourselves, provided we don't wait to see this glorious sunbird all the way out of the egg. Mahindra believes that we'll have at least two E-months' warning, no matter when it happens. That's ample time to take flight."

"What this means," put in Captain Hsi, "is that we may be going home much sooner than any of us expected."

"What's likely to be the impact on Earth, our own solar system?" asked Naomi, shifting in her chair.

"Minimal," Craig said. "We're thirty-seven light-years from home, and we're talking about a nova, a fairly commonplace event in binary systems, and not the life-annihilating bombardment of cosmic rays that would issue from a nearby supernova. Thirty-seven years from now, no one on your Clapham omnibus is even particularly likely to notice."

"Small consolation to the Kybers," Andrik said.

"That's probably right. Even if Onogoro does decouple from Dextro, it's still going to be fried—somewhere out around Laevo, *if* it manages to complete the switchover before Dextro goes nova."

Keiko, shocked, spoke up: "Is there no chance that the planet might survive?"

Craig shook his head, then considered for a moment. "Slim and none, I'd say. The slim is so improbable that to mention it is to give it more notice than it deserves."

"Nevertheless," Keiko urged him.

"All right. If Dextro blazes up precisely when Laevo eclipses its newly recaptured planet, and for a short enough time, maybe—*just maybe*—such a conjunction would protect the Kybers and all their lower-life-form buddies from the main force of the heatwave. And maybe it wouldn't, Kei. Yes or no, there'd still be a whole helluva bunch of charged particles flying around. Even if you could guarantee an eclipse at Fire Time, with Dextro completely occluded from the inhabitants of this world, you couldn't get *me* out on the surface in a deck chair.''

''Maybe the Kybers and the Onogorovan biota could survive,'' Clemencia Venages suggested. ''Maybe they evolved their shells and carapaces and armour for just this sort of situation. I mean, there's a strong body of opinion to the effect that novas fire off every now and then alternately in binaries—because, you know, of gradual matter exchange. So Dextro burns off its excess, and calms down; Laevo builds up its own excess from Dextro's droppings—and eventually it flares too. And so on. Maybe evolution could—''

Craig Olivant grasped the music stand and stared in mute embarrassment at the floor.

Naomi Davis, looking over her shoulder, spoke directly to the young planetologist: ''That isn't something that evolution's likely to take into account. You don't get much chance to recover from the first experience! And it could be millions of years before the repeat performance. No, I'd venture that the shells and whatnot are simply adaptations to the periodic hourglass orbit around the two suns.''

''And now their sands are running out,'' Betti Songa said.

Andrik breathed out wearily. ''We'll have to tell the Kybers.''

''When it's impossible to get through to them?'' Betti asked. ''When, even if we could, there's nothing we can do to help? What's the point in telling them they're condemned . . . to fry?''

"Maybe they already know," Keiko said. She saw again the statues of Kannon in Sanjusangendo and recalled Andrik's fanciful remark about housing the Kybers in such a temple. *Was* it impossible?

Heinrich Eshleman, the chemist, said, "They put up with death rather well, don't they? Rather neatly. Aren't they already 'dead' a great deal of the time?''

"Shut up, Heinrich," Naomi told him.

"We could save a few of them," Andrik said. "If we ferried them up to orbit while they're in kybertrance, what's to prevent us from stacking them like cargo in one of the freight modules?''

"I am," replied Captain Hsi. "We don't have room for that sort of madness, Dr Norn, and the ethics of it are questionable.''

"Whereas the ethics of permitting them all to perish—''

"Hush," Keiko murmured, touching Andrik's hand.

"We could easily save several alien families that way, sir. Maybe as many as a hundred individuals.''

Captain Hsi took the music stand away from Craig. "These possibilities can be dealt with later. In the meantime, to placate your burgeoning sense of responsibility, Dr Norn, I instruct you to discuss with the Kybers this matter of their sun going nova. Do it today if you like.''

"If today is anything like yesterday, sir, or the day before, or the day before that, the Kybers aren't talking.''

"Then perhaps you need some help."

"What sort? I've tried everything I know.''

"Take Dr Takahashi with you. That's a logical step, is it not? If a cyberneticist and a xenologist have no success breaking this annoying impasse, then let a linguist try—especially the linguist who taught one of their number human speech."

"Speech is useless at the graveside," Eshleman remarked wryly, "if you're trying to establish contact with the corpse."

"I would be happy to try," Keiko said. She noted the perplexity in Andrik's gaze as he calculated the odds of her being a genuine help.

"Fine," said Captain Hsi. "In the time remaining to us before our withdrawal, however long from now that may be, I intend to . . ." He began outlining a complex new assignments-schedule, the terms of which altered whimsically with various arcane astrophysical contingencies. Although Keiko struggled to follow the gist of the captain's remarks, her thoughts were already elsewhere . . .

SEVEN

As Andrik of course knew they would, they drew Six-killer as their floater pilot.

Leaving Betti to other tasks in the research complex, they lifted off from the Platform in the floater—a triangular-shaped craft with a semicircular wing and a set of retractable landing legs—in mid-afternoon. The sun, which Keiko could not help viewing with a certain fearful scepticism, hung in the thin Onogorovan atmosphere like a hole burning outward in a piece of violet tissue paper.

The Kyber dwelling nearest the Platform, which had purposely been built above an upland rock face at a remove from the alien palaces, was a good five kilometres distant. The palace of the Kyber whom Andrik and Betti had brought back with them for language lessons lay another kilometre or so beyond that one. Although a team might have easily walked to the nearest inhabited craters, Captain Hsi permitted no one to venture on foot more than a few dozen metres from the base of the Platform.

Floaters were safer. They were equipped with radios,

food, bedding, medicine, and research aids. Moreover, the terrain—where fogs drifted like calving icebergs; where plants sometimes resembled boulders, and boulders plants—made hiking perilous. Crater-probing was an enterprise only for the trained or the sure-of-foot. That was why Sixkiller, in addition to his piloting skills, had earned a place on the Onogoro Expedition, and why Andrik grudgingly suffered his presence on each outing to the rock-strewn plain. Like his reputed ancestors, the man could trailblaze. It was in his blood.

On the brief journey out, Keiko started no conversations with either Andrik or the pilot. Through the parting curtains of mist she studied the landscape, amazed that it should so vividly evoke a battlefield or a meteor-pitted lunar sea. The Kyber palaces—ruins to her inexperienced eye—spread across the entire continent, forming a plurality of septa-communes or perhaps even a single monstrously diffuse metropolis. No one yet knew what sort of social structure the alien population shared, if, indeed, it was not a mere hodgepodge of seven-unit duchies. No one yet knew *anything* very telling about the Kybers, and Sixkiller apparently knew all he wanted to know . . .

"*Outside,*" he had said, "*I keep my mouth shut, and I do my job.*" That, Keiko reflected, seemed to be literally true. Piloting, he was as mute as a stone.

Andrik, perhaps to break the embarrassing silence, said, "The Kyber palaces always remind me of a part of Pompeii redesigned by a psychologist of distorted rooms—Ames, say, or the artist Escher. It would be nice if we could put down right in the middle of a labyrinth's central court, but we'd probably crumple one or more of our hosts."

Lowering the floater's landing legs, Sixkiller

dropped them toward a ridge overlooking one of the alien dwellings. Ice glittered in the rocks. Huge frost mandalas shone forth from the eroded plateaus between the craters, and inside the crater toward which they were falling Keiko saw the canted maze-walls of the approach corridor spiralling inward to the palace atrium. Why no roof? The absence of a roof seemed to make a mockery of the walls meandering about the trapezoidal court at the crater's centre—a misty open space *very* like an Ames distortion chamber, Keiko thought, although considerably larger. But because of the floater's angle of descent and the fog clinging to the walls of the labyrinth, it was impossible to see any of the aliens who supposedly lay comatose at its heart. Then the floater swept across the palace and settled into the rocks on spidery legs. They were down.

Balanced on the ridge overlooking the dwelling, bundled in their parkas and boots, the three of them surveyed the Kyber "ruins."

"This is where you found my student?" Keiko asked.

Andrik nodded, and Sixkiller, with a kind of deadly insouciance, unholstered the laser on his hip and fired at a nearby outcropping of violet quartz. The "quartz" burst open, releasing several puffs of steam and revealing a fleshy core of seed pods or floral placentae. These immediately withered. The smell issuing from the outcropping was, yes, distinctly vinegary. One of the creatures that Naomi called snailies—a vermilion-and-cream shell with a foot like a velvet grey slipper—rolled away from the lithoid plant, and Sixkiller put it in his sights, too.

"Leave it alone," Andrik warned him.

Sixkiller put the laser away, and the snailie rolled

another several metres through the icy groundcover of rocks and rock-like vegetation before slipping over the edge.

Keiko turned to Andrik. "How do *we* get down there? And once down, how do we get inside?"

"Leave that to Sixkiller. There are a number of alternative entrances around the crater. Once you've entered, though, it's very easy to get lost and start inadvertently backtracking. One day, at another Kyber dwelling, we never did make it to the central chamber."

"Milius was your pilot that day," Sixkiller said. "Not me."

"I know, I know. Show Kei your thread of Ariadne, Sixkiller, the trailblazer's infallible aid."

Pokerfaced inside his bulky hood, the pilot held up a phosphor-pen.

"He marks the walls with that. No harmful effects on the Kyber labyrinth, either. The glow fades in two days' time. Captain Hsi and the Luna Port authorities don't want us defacing ancient monuments."

Keiko smiled. How could you deface ruins? A historic building was simply an idea. The Japanese tore down the great shrine at Ise every ten years and built another one, which the people then regarded as of equal historic worth as the preceding structure.

"Let's get down there," Sixkiller said impatiently.

He led them along the edge of the plateau, past ice-riven boulders and over carpets of pebblelike succulents that hissed when they stepped on them. As they scrambled down the slope to the outer wall in the crater, Dextro disappeared in the mist. To compensate, Sixkiller began marking the unmortared wall with the phosphor-pen: streaks of fuzzy, wavering blue in the gloom. Following him and peering ahead for some sign of an opening inward, Keiko shuddered. How could a being with the demonstrable intelligence of her former student hail from such a place? It was cold, colder than on the ridge, and more humid to boot. That she could no longer see their floater was scarcely reassuring, and the sound of crackling laceworks of ice in the sluggish mist continually startled her, too.

"Here," Sixkiller said.

The rubble under Keiko's feet gave way to a floor resembling great shattered flagstones. Gestured forward by the pilot, she and Andrik squeezed through an arch into the outermost spiral of the approach corridor. Fog coiled off the floor, as if somewhere under the surface a Kyber were operating a mist-generator and venting the stuff upward through the cracks in the flagstones. Only Sixkiller's phosphor marks provided any clue to their relative whereabouts inside the maze.

"Now you know how a frog must feel," Andrik murmured.

"A frog?" asked Keiko.

"All it can perceive is dark edges, or sustained contrasts, or maybe net darkening. That's it."

Sixkiller halted and turned back on them. "And you suppose the Kybers as far above us in their perceptiveness as we are above frogs—is that it, Dr Norn?"

"That's entirely possible, Sixkiller," Andrik replied fiercely. "But we're never going to know if you don't get us where we're supposed to go."

The pilot hesitated. Keiko feared that he was on the verge of mutiny. What would they do if he left them to their own devices and returned to the Platform without them, swearing that she and Andrik had fallen victim to the terrain or to the unexpected rapacity of the resurrected Kybers? He might well be believed. . . .

Dextro, a muted fireball, reappeared overhead. As

soon as the mist had swaddled it again, Sixkiller
scowled contemptuously and turned back to his task. In
a moment he was several metres ahead of them, trailing
phosphor marks by way of recrimination and duty.

"Bastard," grumbled Andrik.

Another fifteen minutes in the corridor, sometimes
moving inward through irregularly spaced arches, Sixkiller at last led them into the atrium. An open space,
thought Keiko, grateful to have been delivered from the
claustrophobic possibilities of the maze. An open
space.

The mist at her back parted, whipped upward in a
gust of wind, and waved dissolving grey tendrils at the
sky. There was Dextro again. It loomed in the ill-woven
fog like a Chinese lantern, fat and corrugated and
orange.

What Keiko saw in the chamber struck her as forcibly
as if she had entered a charnelhouse.

Six Kybers occupied the trapezoidal atrium, two
lying together on a bierlike stone slab, one frozen in a
ridiculous squatting posture, two elevated on their extensible legs to a stationary height of nearly three
metres, and a final one sitting in a corner on a nonexis-
tent chair. Mortuary statues? Skeletons? Metallic
mummies? The sight was chilling. Nothing moved but
a few tatters of mist. The aura of death so permeated the
open chamber that Keiko's first inclination was to flee
back the way she had come.

But she held her ground and asked the obvious question: "Where's the seventh Kyber, Andrik?"

"Are there only six?" He made a quick count. "One
of them's out and about, sure enough. Your student, I
think."

"How do you know which is which?"

"I don't," Andrik confessed. "I can't tell the Kybers apart any better than I can Orientals."

"You sometimes confuse me with Captai Hsi, then?"

Andrik, who had been smiling, enjoying the banter, suddenly caught himself up and looked at the floater pilot. "No," he said, "but Sixkiller occasionally does."

Sixkiller, his doe's eyes utterly tranquil, drew his hand laser and pointed it at one of the Kybers. "Only six," he said. "Today, Dr Norn, I could prove the appropriateness of my name."

"Farrell!" Keiko exclaimed, reaching toward him.

Effortlessly, the floater pilot sidestepped her and aimed the weapon at the Kyber enthroned on thin air. He fired. Pivoting, he fired at each of the remaining five aliens, deliberately missing every one of them. Tiny plumes of smoke or steam curled out of the walls that had intercepted his laser shots.

Andrik lunged at the man. "Goddamn you, Sixkiller—!"

Again the floater pilot casually stepped aside, holstering his weapon as he did so. "If they weren't already dead, that is. If they just weren't already dead."

Keiko gripped Sixkiller by the shoulder, surprising him, and thrust him back with all her might. "Then why is one of them not here?" she demanded. "If they're already dead, how has one managed to leave its tomb and go wandering about on Onogoro like a living creature?"

"Like your lover's hoped-for saviour, you mean!"

Andrik brushed Keiko aside, and she watched in alarm as the xenologist jockeyed the pilot back into the approach corridor and up against one of its walls.

"Go back to the floater, Sixkiller. Go back to the floater and report your trigger-happy behaviour and my disapproval of it to Captain Hsi." Then Andrik let go of the man and stepped back.

Sixkiller looked neither abashed nor defiant. "If you think it'll do any good," he said. He unhooked his utility belt—with its laser, ration packets, and phosphor-pen, among other items—and handed it to Andrik. "You may be able to use some of these things, if you're going to stay here without me."

Then, as the xenologist had commanded, Sixkiller headed into the fog of the approach corridor, ostensibly on his way back to the floater. Keiko again found herself wondering what would happen if he deserted them. . . .

EIGHT

Andrik gestured at the aliens. There they are, the gesture implied; do what you can to break their kyber-trance.

Keiko approached the nearer of the two standing figures and stared up into its lofty face. Perhaps she would do better to begin with a more accessible family representative. So, after strolling bemusedly among the frozen possibilities, she halted before the Kyber enthroned on air. It looked almost exactly like the alien she had tutored in the knowledge centre. But, then, so did all the others in the chamber, if you disregarded minor variations in the colours of their eye patches or in the shapes of their halo-crests. Otherwise, the Kybers conformed to a highly standardized pattern. Did that fact corroborate Sixkiller's assembly-line hypothesis?

Keiko turned to Andrik, now only a step or two behind her. "I don't even have a name," she said. "I don't know how to begin."

"Just talk to it."

Sceptical and embarrassed, Keiko reached out and touched one of the creature's rigid arms.

"Don't!" Andrik shouted.

The arm reacted to her touch by swinging like a lethal boom, swiftly and soundlessly. Keiko leapt away. The arm swung back to its original position and locked.

"Didn't I warn you about that?" Andrik asked. "A touch is a dangerous stimulus. Just speak to it, Kei."

Heartened rather than dismayed (since even an automatic movement implied the possibility of life), Keiko took up a stance directly in front of the alien and leaned forward to tell it a secret.

"Kyber," she whispered. "Kyber, I am Keiko Takahashi, and I taught you the language of humanity."

A wind blew over the pit, making melancholy music. Keiko, Andrik, and the six rigid Kybers were *inside* this wail. Her whisper was muffled by the sound, and the alien did not move.

"Louder," Andrik advised her.

In competition with the wind she said, "I am Keiko Takahashi, and I taught you the—"

"You taught me a phonic system of communication," said a lilting soprano voice behind her. Both she and Andrik spun about to see one of the two elevated Kybers collapsing upon its stiltlike legs somewhat nearer to human height. Still gigantic, it tottered forward as if to corral them in the chamber's corner with the seated alien. "That is, you taught me through your tutoring of our former prime, who has spread the word in mind and person to neighbouring families."

Keiko and Andrik retreated, only to find that the Kyber behind them was rearing out of its seated posture in a single, continuous, gravity-defying movement. Without even shifting its feet it hoisted itself erect, then telescoped to the same towering height as that of the

Kyber who had just spoken. Within a matter of seconds three other aliens had also come to life. Only the two lying back to back on the stone slab against the trapezoidal chamber's rear wall remained in their death-coma.

"Then you're not my student?" asked Keiko to the first resurrectee, mindful of her and Andrik's puniness and isolation.

"We are *all* your student," said the Kyber whose arm had nearly struck her. "Your voice is therefore familiar to us. Upon your addressing us forthrightly, Lady Keiko, we arise and sing."

The three later risers crowded up behind the first resurrectee. Piped one, "Though I have never sat down with you in the knowledge centre and drilled for hours in the rudiments of Translic, I am still your student."

"As am I," echoed the second newcomer.

"As am I," sang the third.

They hovered above and about the two human beings like impossibly large mechanized statues, distorted figures from a nightmare or a drug fugue. Despite the profound depth of the kybertrance from which they had just awakened, they seemed lively and curious. Further in the last ten seconds, they had volunteered more information about themselves than had Keiko's absent dropout in nearly fifty Onogorovan days.

"You are all her student?" asked Andrik of the clustering aliens, one hand on Keiko's arm.

"Indeed," crooned the first resurrectee. "All of us, in the most encompassing sense." To suggest every inhabited crater on the plain, its arm swept theatrically around the horizon of the sheltering ruins. A learned gesture, Keiko realized, a visual aid akin to Olivant's clumsy ellipses or even the absentminded choreography of her own small hands . . .

"Every Kyber on Onogoro now has the capacity to speak Translic?" exclaimed Andrik. "Don't tell me you're telepathic!"

"Request granted," said the family's designated mouthpiece.

"No," cried Andrik, chopping with his hand. "Tell me! While in kybertrance you're all in subconscious—or is it *para*conscious—contact with one another: isn't that it? Resonating minds? Conjoined consciousness?"

The four resurrected Kybers gaped, not without a certain deliberate irony, it seemed to Keiko. She noticed, too, that the lateral pupils of the creatures—now nearly twice their normal size—were glowing brightly. Occasionally, in fact, an alien would turn its great head in order to view them with a peripheral eye-bulb , as if attempting to shine into their very souls a psychic ophthalmoscope.

"Why couldn't you speak to Andrik or Betti or Farrell?" she asked. "What made you wait for me?"

"We are *your* student," said the first to awaken.

"But I might never have come. This is the only time I've ever actually threaded my way into one of your dwellings. My principal work is on the Platform."

"We were waiting for the lessons you bring."

"The only lesson she brings," said Andrik, looking at the parodically saintly faces of the aliens, "is that any of us might have carried. Your bloody sun is going to explode!"

"Dextro—pejoratively bloody—in actual fact radiates principally between angstrom units—" The alien stopped, canted its head. "But let us not speak technically, Lady Keiko. The lesson you bring is lost neither in its transport nor upon us at its arrival. We have anticipated it and learned it by heart. The recitation of our knowledge is what we have held in reserve for your coming.''

Andrik, at a loss, turned to Keiko. "They say they know.''

"Evidently.''

The xenologist pointed skyward. "You realize that Onogoro is going to decouple from Dextro because of the heavy inner planet? That Laevo may or may not recapture your world? That Dextro itself will inevitably flare up and eject shells of annihilating gas at huge velocity? You genuinely understand the seriousness of the situation?''

"In all its gravity,'' replied the family speaker.

"But you joke, you pun,'' cried Andrik, a titbird strutting before Titans. "The truth of the matter is that your world is doomed and your people with it!''

"In such circumstances,'' crooned the Kyber, "it would seem essential to appeal to a higher power.''

Andrik's expression was incredulous. "How? By prayer?''

"*Orare est laborare.* Our prayer is our labour. Oratory in the laboratory of our souls.''

"You're going to pray that some higher power shunts Onogoro into a viable orbit around Laevo? And your prayer is going to bring about the very orbit your people desire?''

"We pray to ourselves, Lady Keiko,'' said the alien, ignoring Andrik. "Each of us is a god in turn. We all worship the septa-prime, whom each will become turn by turn in the cycle of our apotheosis.''

"Apotheosis?''

"I speak now not of kybertrance, but of the ordinary social world we share with you at present.''

Confused, Keiko nodded at the aliens lying back to back on their slate-grey bier. "Are they also gods— intermittently?''

"Even they, who maintain us in underlinkage and

psalm in death-sleep a versicle of our people's common prayer.''

"You can't move worlds by psalms or magic,'' Andrik protested. "The *Heavenbridge* isn't terribly large, but—''

"Should we fear its want of largeness, Lady Keiko, or the wiles of human largesse?''

"Damn it!''Andrik overrode both the Kyber and her. "If you'll switch yourselves off—go into kyber-trance, or hibernation, or whatever it is—we can take a hundred or more of you to safety with us.''

"Perhaps,'' cautioned Keiko.

"To our own world, thirty-seven lights from here, a place of safety.'' Andrik pointed heavenward, grimaced. "It's one of the tragedies of the universe that over aeons a sapient species arises only to be obliterated by a—by a cockeyed cosmic accident,'' he concluded bitterly.

A Kyber behind the family speaker looked into the mists concealing Dextro and intoned. "Nothing is accidental, everything meshes, deaths are significant, life has a cause.''

"But the conjunction of life with an event that crassly annihilates it,'' Andrik declared, "*is* an accident!''

"Part of the plan of a star,'' said the family speaker. "As for the plan of our planet, we shall walk in the sheen and the shadow of Laevo, sun-shadow our shield.''

"As Craig said was possible,'' Keiko reminded Andrik, "the new sun blocking the blast of the old.''

"But what's to guarantee such an alignment?'' Andrik protested. "You *have* no guarantee.''

"Throughout the community of families, we read the signatures of suns and decipher their messages.''

Keiko wondered if this were possible. Humanity had long had experimental syntheses of the organic and the mechanical: the brain and the computer interfacing, disabled limbs co-operating with sophisticated prosthetics, mechanical systems exploiting the advantages of sensory plug-ins. But would a human being ever be able to *see* the solar wind, or X-rays, or the fabric of meta-space? The Kybers had apparently grown into these capabilities, evolved into them, maybe even restructured themselves along biomechanical lines to achieve this condition of heightened awareness. What hope was there for humanity to do likewise?

"Are you born or made?" Keiko asked impulsively, thinking of Sixkiller and his implacable hostility toward the aliens.

"Born," sang the family speaker. "Born, born, born; born in Bethlehem. Each crater a cradle, each maze a manger. Like you and your gods, the Kybers are born."

"But you're all adults," Keiko said. "Where are the children? Don't you have to grow into adulthood?"

"Of course we must grow." The Kyber suddenly elevated itself another half metre, then slid smoothly back to its previous height. "The child is father to the clan. There have been no children among us since a hundred revolutions after Onogoro's last decoupling from Laevo. But, Lady Keiko, after our departure from this unstable orbit there will be children again."

"Your birth cycles—your gestation periods—correspond to the times of transit between the two suns?" Andrik looked at Keiko, then back at the complacent alien. "That means you have children no more often than every—what?—every couple of thousand years."

"Blessed events," said the Kyber laconically.

"And damn rare ones," Andrik replied. "With such a birth rate how do you manage to replace those among you who die? Or don't your people die?"

"Frequently," the Kyber responded. "We all die frequently."

"Are you immortal, then? Are these 'little deaths' a means of defeating Death itself?"

"They are a means of knowing," the alien said.

Keiko watched Andrik pace among the four resurrected Kybers, scrutinizing their faces and trying in vain to control his excitement. Each time he looked back at her, his eyes glinted with Dextro light and the set of his lips bespoke either triumph or a long-deferred vindication. He seemed alternately smug and chastened—but it was also clear that he felt genuine gratitude for what she had helped him accomplish, whatever that was. Lady Keiko, his eyes told her, you have proved yourself as alien and admirable as the Onogorovans. And yet, in truth, she had little understanding of what she had done . . .

"Of knowing what?" Andrik asked. "The secrets of your sun's life cycle? The answer to the riddle of ultimate meaning? If you can't tell us *what* you know, tell us *how* to know what you know."

The family's speaker tottered away from its human questioners, stared ritually skyward, then dropped its wall-eyed gaze back upon both Andrik and Keiko. Its lateral pupils had swollen to the size and colour of overripe grapes; the tatters of sailcloth flesh draping its polelike arms popped in the wind like firecrackers.

"Impossible," it told them. "To tell you is probably impossible. But to *show* you, yes, that remains an option."

NINE

Keiko and Andrik stayed in the Kyber palace for nearly three more hours, explaining, arguing, gawking. One of the items on Sixkiller's utility belt was a miniature recording unit, and Andrik used it to preserve the arcane pronouncements of the family speaker. For the most part, the alien's one- or two-line speeches had either the puzzling succinctness of *koans,* Zen riddles propounded by a living machine, or the dour flavour of bad puns indifferently peddled and garnished. The longer they stayed among the Kybers, in fact, the more amazed Keiko grew at the dearth of real information conveyed by these pronouncements—if, indeed, she and Andrik were not simply too obtuse to extract from them their intricately encoded meanings. Maybe the cold had something to do with the seeming unintelligibility of the Kyber aphorisms. In any case, after the first hour of interrogation and badinage, two of the aliens suddenly dropped back into kybertrance, freezing where they stood, and a third stalked out of the atrium into the encircling labyrinth. Twilight wove its way through the fog, and the wind picked up.

"Let us take you off this planet before your sun flares

up,'' Andrik pleaded for the tenth or twelfth time.
''Some of you, at least.''

''Your offer to turn the *Heavenbridge* into Noah's
Ark is undoubtedly well intentioned,'' warbled the
family speaker. ''But the 'safety' toward which you
would steer us would be—perhaps—inimical to our
essence. Moreover, you do not truly understand
steersmanship, by which we mean the controlled direction of a process.''

''What process?''

''Thought and metathought, world and metaworld,
cosmos and metacosmos. Your eyes still do not permit
you to peer over the threshold of This-Reality, Dr Norn.
You are as yet unconjoined with your machines.''

''Tell me how—''

''Laevo rises soon, and you must return to your
Platform. Visit us at the Rite of Conjoining, when we
adjure again the influence of Dextro and remake ourselves according to the precepts of a different light.''

The Kyber swivelled its head, elevated itself eigh-
teen or twenty centimetres, then abruptly shut down all
visible organic operation. Keiko and Andrik were alone
again with the unmoving husks of several alien intelligences. The Kyber that had earlier departed, walking
out as if in a fit of impatience or pique, still had not
come back. Andrik turned off the portable recording
unit and signalled that he was finally ready to leave;
there was little more they were likely to learn today, and
Sixkiller had probably just about given up on them.

Guided by the markings of the pilot's phosphor-pen,
they retraced their path through the Kyber labyrinth.
Keiko was silent. It was too cold either to think or to
talk.

Once out of the maze, they clambered up the steep,
shadow-etched bank of the crater. Atop the ridge, forty

or fifty metres distant, perched their floater, resembling a great, silver wasp. Dextro was setting, and Laevo had positioned itself low on the horizon, a hard little circle pouring bone-white radiance through the mists. More startling to Keiko was the apparition of two Kybers hovering in silhouette beside their floater, like medieval saints on stilts. She and Andrik exchanged a surprised glance, and together they hurried across the ridge to see what was happening.

"*Kei ko,*" sang a melodious feminine voice as they approached. "My mentor, my madonna, whose hardness is also mine."

Sixkiller stood between the two aliens, his back pressed against the floater; he appeared to be trying to protect expeditionary property from a threat still not wholly clear to him. His eyes—Keiko saw when they were nearer—were wide with apprehension and resolve. He brightened visibly upon catching sight of them. With choppy gestures he urged them to hurry.

"You've found my student," Keiko told Sixkiller.

"This other one found me," said the floater pilot, looking back and forth between the two Kybers. "And then your—your *student* showed up."

The fingers of the former septa-prime stroked the nose of the aircraft. "This is the one in which I rode, yes?"

"Yes," said Andrik. "Have your people no mechanical transportation of their own?"

"For the most part we travel with our minds," it replied. "Otherwise, our legs do lift us lightly where we wish to go."

"Pistons," said Sixkiller. "Their legs are pistons."

"They've told us that they're born," Keiko heard herself saying. "Not made or engineered, Farrell, but *born.*"

"They took up watch here a while back, that's all I know—first the one, and then the other. Neither the floater's radio nor its pulse engine would operate while they were standing here. Finally—finally I got out and told them to beat it. They didn't budge, they didn't blink."

"You tried to leave us?" Keiko cried.

"Not you, damn it—them! After first attempting to radio."

Keiko's student cocked his head to one side. "I wished to greet you again, Lady Kei. My sibling spouses informed me of your presence in the palace, and this one," nodding at the other Kyber, "came out to divest me of a portion of that which I have foraged on our family's behalf."

At that, the alien removed from a hooklike chip of bone or metal at its waist the carcass of one of the planet's mottled snailies. This it handed past Sixkiller to its sibling, who had already relieved it of several of the glistening shells.

Food, Keiko told herself; food, perhaps, for metathought . . .

"They eat," she said to the floater pilot. "They're born, and they eat. What other proof of their organic nature do you want, Farrell?"

"I don't want any proof. I want to get out of here."

Andrik turned to Keiko's student, who was suddenly the same height as the human beings, its posture both poised and expectant. "What is the Rite of Conjoining?" the xenologist asked. "Just before everyone down there," gesturing toward the crater, "froze up on us again, we were invited to attend a ceremony by that name."

"Yes. Do come. At Onogoro's decoupling."

"But what is it?"

"A sharing of data preparatory to transit. A celebration of conceptions. An obeisance to the forces of delivery."

"It has to do with birth, then?"

"Birth, resurrection, renewal, and life—all at strata of consciousness inaccessible to the unconjoined."

"Then how the hell are we going to be able to participate?" Sixkiller demanded of Andrik and Keiko. "Do we bring our own extension cords and plug into the nearest faintly humming Kyber?"

The Kyber tore a piece of sailcloth flesh from its right arm and offered it to Sixkiller. "Eat thou this in remembrance of what thou hast never been," it said, not untenderly.

The floater pilot struck aside the alien's outstretched fingers, cursing beneath his breath. The torn flesh fluttered to the rime-embroidered rocks.

Keiko retrieved the spurned offering and tried to examine it in the failing light. Here was, at last, a long-awaited biosample—even if Sixkiller vandalistically ignored the fact. Actually, it looked no more edible than a canvas boot string. While she inspected it, Sixkiller yanked back the floater's outer hatch, insulted by her attention to such rubbish, and swung himself acrobatically up from the ground to clamber up the recessed steps back into his cockpit.

Andrik scarcely even noted his defection. "Why have you been in kybertrance—death-sleep—these past several days?" he asked, rephrasing a question that the aliens in the labyrinth had pointedly ignored, whatever its wording.

"To conceive of ourselves anew," said the Kyber cryptically. "To issue a programme for transit. To programme our issue for Laevo-light."

Keiko rose from where she had been kneeling. She

had in mind a question so incongruous that it had to be spoken aloud. "Is each of you," she began, "well, *pregnant?*"

"Two of us are," the former septa-prime replied. "The two whom you observed lying in paracybergamic union on the common birthbed. Yes, inseminated with the grace notes of our psalm to the God-Behind-the-Galaxies, they are pregnant with data. And in every septa-commune, Lady Keiko, are two such pregnant Kybers linked in death-sleep for the long gestation."

"And linked, too," surmised Andrik, a sweep of his hand taking in the vast, forbidding landscape of the Kyber plain, "with every other death-sleeping member of your species, no matter where they are."

"We must go," the alien told him. "Awaiting our return are four who hunger and two who process information toward its most apt embodiment."

"A Kyber infant? One to each family; a child with two dams and at least five sires? Or should that be 'processers' and 'programmers', conception among you being at least as much an intellectual as a sexual act?"

"Good night, Lady Kei." The former septa-prime instantly regained its most imposing height. With the other Kyber picking its way after, it tottered along the ridge toward the sunken palace. Two metallic storks on a rocky beach, at length disappearing down into their citadel of stones.

Impulsively Keiko tasted the strip of flesh from her former student's arm. It was bitter, alumlike, its texture reminiscent of chewing-gum or pickled octopus. It flavoured her saliva with alien molecules. Before she could spit the taste away, a thin gruel of Onogorovan trace elements slid down her throat. Then, at last, she spat, wiped her mouth with the back of her mitten, and plunged the remaining bit of kyberflesh into the pouch on her parka.

Andrik laughed mirthlessly. "You're going to save that? As a memento? After the way it apparently tasted?"

"Think, Andrik." Keiko glared at the xenologist, wondering at a mind that could soar after ultimate truths but blithely overlook the essential details of daily field work. "I'm going to give this to Eshleman and Naomi. For analysis. In all the time we've been here, we've never had from the Kybers the equivalent of even a fingernail clipping to put under our microscopes."

The bitter taste lingered in her mouth. She waited for pastel optical illusions to bloom in her head, for a fire like liquid ice to flicker across the membranes of her gut. Neither of these things happened.

The taste faded, a memory in her nostrils.

"Of course," Andrik said. But he had spoken with archangels, and his smile was as distant as it was seraphic.

They flew back to the Platform as earlier that day they had flown out to the Onogorovan plain—in a mutually enforced silence.

TEN

Seven days passed, a week if you counted by Earthly standards and ignored the fact that Onogoro had no moon but Il Penseroso.

The examination of the bit of kyberflesh that Keiko had brought back revealed that its cellular composition resembled that of human skin, at least insofar as the presence of chromosomes and nucleic acid went. Even thirty-seven light-years from home, DNA was DNA—a fact that Naomi Davis and Heinrich Eshleman had already confirmed with their experiments on other local life forms. Still, certain anomalies and differences did exist.

In addition to the helical DNA molecules in the nucleus of each Kyber cell—molecules that, teased out to full length, would have made a strand nearly four times as long as those coiled in a human cell—Naomi and Heinrich found minute, free-floating latticework structures that Keiko's friend dubbed "cryptosomes", all of which possessed crystaloid properties. What were these tiny crystals doing at the heart of that most basic of all organic units, the cell? Not even the snailies and the mock-tortoises of the planet had exhibited such an arrangement at this fundamental level, whether their cell samples were scraped from the fleshy portions of their bodies or chipped from their organic shells. In this respect, then, the Kybers were different from every other life form whose genetic biology had come under the scrutiny of expeditionary scientists. But because the cryptosomes in the Kyber cells appeared to be inert bodies without identifiable purpose or function, Naomi was at a loss to explain the *meaning* of the difference.

"It must have *something* to do with the way they are," Keiko said, treading water in the big, plastic tub braced beneath the decking of the Platform's bathhouse. Overhead, through a taut polyethylene film, the interthreading pinks and violets of an alien sunset.

Naomi was opposite her in the languidly swirling water, both arms extended along a support rail. "Oh, assuredly," she replied, her face flushed and her eyes bright with decaying fatigue. "Here are creatures who seem to be made half of skin and half of old clothes hangers and aluminium closet poles, and they've got neat little crystals swimming around in their cells. It points to a blending of the supposedly unmixable, just as does the outward form of their big, clunking bodies."

"They don't clunk," Keiko corrected Naomi gently.

"No? Well, perhaps they don't. Heinrich thinks the cryptosomes may be evidence in the Kyber physiology of some sort of insidious environmental contaminant. Yes. A contaminant having to do with Dextro's getting ready to go nova, he thinks."

"You don't think that?"

Naomi pooched out her lips, comically. "Neither does Heinrich, if you want to know the truth. He's guessing. Everybody's guessing.''

''What's your guess, Naomi?''

''My guess is that the cryptosomes have a great deal to do with the reproduction of Kyber body cells and maybe even that of Kyber individuals. In fact, I think cryptosomes—which, by the by, haven't done diddly for us in the laboratory, even though that bit of skin you brought us isn't really dead yet—yes, well, the cryptosomes just may replicate themselves in the context of DNA replication. They do a little dance together.''

''Crystals and nucleic acid?'' asked Keiko sceptically. ''That isn't possible, is it?''

Naomi closed her eyes, pinched her nostrils together with one hand, and dunked herself. She came up blowing, streaming. Droplets flew from her matted cap of hair, which she shook from side to side. ''Whew! Wow!'' She opened her eyes; diamonds dripped down her lashes, and her pupils contracted to graphite points.

''Not on our own bonny green planet,'' she managed. ''So far as we know. But out here, Keiko, out here I think the four different nitrogen compounds in DNA somehow affect the atomic bonding capabilities of the cryptosomes and draw them into heredity's pretty helical molecule. Once in there, why, they're part of the programme. They dictate inherited characteristics just as do the adenine-thymine and cytosine-guanine matchups. That's what I think.''

''I don't understand that.''

''Neither do I. But it's interesting that there are four nitrogen compounds in DNA and four types of latticework bondings among crystals, don't you think? Let Earthbound geneticists smirk—the Kybers' cellular biology suggests they've evolved a means to encode so much inheritable data in a single skin cell that all the libraries and knowledge centres ever built couldn't hold a fraction of it, not even in their combined microfiche files.''

''Naomi!'' Keiko caught the rail behind her and hung on to it with one hand.

''I'm not exaggerating. Not much, anyway.''

''Why such complexity? The Kybers are human scale, relatively speaking. They certainly aren't planet-sized creatures with oceans for brains and mountains for backbones. Some of that cellular information must be redundant.''

''Indeed. And think of the possibility for genetic mistakes, for mutations, considering all these half-way-to-infinite base-pair steps, each one asterisked with some sort of niggling cryptosomatic footnote. Criminy!'' Naomi, like a child in a wading pool, put her face into the water and snorted horsily. Gasping she bobbed back up shaking her short sodden grey tresses. ''Incredible that they're all so uniform in appearance, isn't it?''

Keiko took up a piece of bathing pumice and rubbed it between her breasts. ''As if they've come off an assembly line. Which is just what Sixkiller continues to claim—in spite of the living flesh I gave you and their own counterclaim that they're born.'' She smiled wistfully. ''Born in Bethlehem; every one of them a god.''

''Well, maybe the seeming redundancy of all that genetic information isn't a redundancy at all, Kei. Only a portion of it goes to dictating their physical makeup, say, while the remainder—the majority, I'd bet—encodes data about everything from the devil to the deep blue sea.''

Despite the soothing roil of the waters, Keiko's pulse quickened. She recalled that Andrik had once spun out a brief fantasy about the aliens using kybertrance to process the data with which their waking lives periodically overloaded them. *Data*. Like a marked card or a dud coin, that word kept turning up. And Andrik— well, the last time they had spent the night together had been the night of the thousand shimmering bodhisattvas of Mercy, before their first joint outing to the plain.

Since then, well, he had hurt her . . .

"Data?" she heard herself echo Naomi.

"Absolutely. It's a kind of paradox, really. The Kybers may have incorporated extrasomatic data— facts, if you like—into their cellular physiology. Of course, those encoded facts wouldn't be worth a brass farthing if the Kybers didn't also have some innate means of breaking the code and encompassing its information intellectually. Which they do. Kybertrance is probably the biological agency of the transfer."

"Andrik said something like that a week ago."

"Andrik's very sharp, Kei. He damn well understands the Kybers at least as well as he does himself . . . or you."

Keiko tossed the bathing pumice on the decking and eased herself out into the centre of the tub, her heart a hammer under her naked breast.

"Sorry," apologized Naomi off-handedly. "Did Andrik also say that a Kyber infant must be born a veritable genius by human standards?"

"No." She released the word grudgingly, not wanting even to think about what Andrik had or had not said.

"That's where the genetic aspect comes in, you see. Compared with the Kybers, a human baby is a blank piece of paper ready to be written on, nobody knowing whether it's going to be given over to scribbles or elegant heroic couplets. From the outset, though, a Kyber baby is an encyclopedia of extrasomatic data just waiting to be applied to the challenges of life in its particular bailiwick, meaning, of course, the Gemini system. It holds its experience in common with every other Kyber.''

Keiko finned herself about. ''Challenges like switching back and forth between suns every few thousand years? Challenges like Dextro's getting ready to go nova?''

'''Well, that's the situation, isn't it? Still, I think one of the Kybers' biggest challenges may have been the advent of the *Heavenbridge* and all us twitchy creatures who jumped down from it in hopes of understanding them. That's why one of them came to us for language lessons, through which it also absorbed a smacking lot of human history, literature, and scientific thought. Their metabolisms may require abstract data at least as much as they do organic foodstuffs.''

''You make them sound—once in possession of the necessary amounts of data—sufficient unto themselves.'' Keiko, again treading water, faced the middle-aged ecologist, relishing her own buoyancy and studying Naomi's amiable, puttylike features. ''But when we went down to the Kyber palace last week, one of them talked about appealing to a higher power.''

''I listened to the tape, you know.''

''Yes, I guess you did. But to what sort of 'higher power' would a knowledgeable species like the Kybers appeal?''

''The most proper one, I'd wager,'' said Naomi Davis, bobbing up and down while submerging herself no deeper than her chins. Under the water her breasts lifted and fell languidly. ''They talked of prayers and souls and suchlike, didn't they?''

''My former student even mentioned a 'God-Behind-the-Galaxies', but we weren't recording then.''

"Well," said Naomi, ceasing to bob.

So oddly inflected was this word that Keiko and Naomi burst into grins. Tension seeped out of the muscles in Keiko's lower back, and the warm water suddenly had a womblike cosiness. Andrik, whom she genuinely loved, had never made her feel as comfortable and serene as had dowdy Naomi Davis with a single ambiguous syllable . . ."

"What else didn't get recorded?" Naomi asked.

"That the Kyber infant has seven parents and issues from the bodies of two rather than merely one of this number. But, of course, they can't all contribute genetical material." Keiko grinned again. "Can they?"

"Who knows? I'd bet that the two birth-parents provide the stuff of heredity while the others act as guides, shaping that stuff in kybertrance. Maybe this superredundant control system is what ensures that the umpity-billion base-pair steps of their DNA replication don't go awry and result in mutations or aborted Kyber foetuses. That could also explain why they all look so deucedly much alike, in spite of the chances for biological snafus."

"And why there are so few of them, too."

"Absolutely." Naomi dog-paddled toward Keiko, swinging her head from side to side—an outright amateur at water sports. Then she halted. Treading in place after having swum only a couple of body lengths, she tried to catch her breath. "Which—altogether—solves the mystery of—the Kybers," she wheezed reaching for Keiko's shoulder. "Let's talk—talk about—something—important."

"Very well." Keiko caught the older woman and supported her under the arms while scissoring gently with her feet. Their naked bodies were a hand apart, but the water circulating about and between them was a unifying bond. "Like what, Naomi? Astrophysics? Religion? Politics?"

"No, no. Like—like Andrik, Kei."

"There's nothing to talk about." Keiko released the older woman and averted her face. "The Kybers have 'died' again. Andrik goes out every day looking for one who will awaken to his voice, and nothing happens. Four days ago I went back with him to the crater of my former student, to see if I couldn't trigger one or more of them into consciousness—*our* kind of consciousness—and that didn't work, either." She looked back at Naomi. "I am not Prince Charming, nor was meant to be."

Naomi laughed appreciatively. "Neither is he, dear. Heaven to Hades, Kei, neither is your Andrik."

"Well, he would stay out there overnight if Captain Hsi would permit it. Farrell says that Andrik goes to the centre of a different labyrinth every day and perches in the atrium like a naturalist hoping to observe some rare bird, muttering 'Kyber, Kyber' at intervals and staring at the statuary as if hypnotized. On the day I went with them, Farrell said, he was better, the whole trip was better—because we abandoned my student's atrium fairly quickly and went to three others before returning to the Platform. Betti has stopped going altogether. She says that this is a 'down' period for the Kybers, and there's nothing new to be learned until decoupling."

"They're preparing for switchover and controlling the gestation processes of their conjoined mothers."

"Growing babies—little Kyber Newtons and Einsteins—who will die when Dextro blazes up, along with all the rest of them." Keiko swam back to the edge of the tub, folded her arms on the decking, and put her forehead on her wrists. "That's why Andrik—" She stopped.

"Why he's given himself completely to the aliens—at the expense of his own mental well being and his relationships with people. Yes, I know. And you, Kei, are not least among those who have suffered."

ELEVEN

"Time's up!" shouted a male voice from the entrance to the bathhouse. "Time's up, ladies! Your time's up!"

Keiko turned around, and Naomi dog-paddled to a railing near the door. Through it came Farrell Sixkiller in rubber flip-flops and a blue terry-cloth robe; behind him, similarly dressed, sauntered Captain Hsi, his eyes passing noncommittally over the surface of the tub and the heads of the two women.

"Your reservations for the bathhouse were for thirty minutes," said Sixkiller, looking at Keiko. "Captain Hsi has only fifteen to enjoy the water, I'm afraid, and your time is up."

"Well, I'm gone," said Naomi Davis cheerfully enough. "In any case, I'm turned to a prune, and you're welcome to it." She found a ladder and hoisted herself to the decking, her rump and midriff quivering as if they might at any moment detach themselves and slide into the water. Sixkiller helped her gain a firm purchase on the floor and handed her a towel.

"They need not leave," said Captain Hsi, smiling,

formally and blinking at the darkening sky. "It is quite a large tub, after all."

But Keiko, aware that his courtesy was rote and basically unsympathetic, also hurried to exit the tub, murmuring her own rote courtesies about the captain's kindness. Besides, he perhaps deserved a few moments of solitude under relaxing circumstances; this had not been a good week for him, either. Of course, it appeared that Farrell was going to share these fifteen minutes with him, and that likelihood also demanded that she and Naomi withdraw. The bathhouse was not customarily a trysting place, but neither was it necessarily a place of abstinence. Keiko thought again of Andrik's description of the floater pilot as the satellite of an unstable binary consisting of the captain and young Clemencia. Apparently Sixkiller was still in orbit about the former, if, indeed, he had *ever* swung out of the man's cold and encompassing shadow.

Keiko's towel lay on a bench beneath the polyethylene dome. She retrieved it and pulled it about herself sari-fashion. Naomi was already on the way out, and she did not wish to be left behind with Sixkiller and his praetorian lover. They were often less than pleasant company.

"Wait," said the floater pilot, approaching and taking Keiko's arm. "Please stay. You've heard the captain say he doesn't mind if you remain. Isn't that right, sir?"

A slight lifting of that Pekinese snout seemed to second Sixkiller's assessment of the matter, but the fact that Captain Hsi said nothing more aloud confirmed Keiko in her feeling that she was unwelcome.

"No, thank you," She looked at Sixkiller quizzically. "Is Andrik back?"

"If I am, he is—isn't he?" Knowing that she would

not stay, he tightened his grip on her elbow and wrist, then turned as if to escort her after Naomi. ''I'll be right back, sir. Go ahead and enjoy your bath.''

On their way to the adjacent dressing chamber, a carpeted area with benches and open lockers, Keiko, glancing back into the dome, saw Captain Hsi raise his eyebrows at her cryptically and then shed his bathrobe with a graceful shrugging of his shoulders. Then, the splash of his dive.

Naomi was in the dressing chamber, pulling on a pleated, loose-fitting tunic and a pair of pleated gold trousers. ''Don't worry,'' she told the floater pilot. ''I'm leaving again.'' After massaging her scalp vigorously with her fingertips, she waved off Keiko's plea to remain, gathered up a wet towel and a pair of red and gold slippers, and disappeared into the corridor.

''What do you want?'' Keiko demanded.

''You asked about Andrik—Dr Norn, I mean. Well, today's watchword, Dr Takahashi, is 'Time's up'. Time is up on a number of fronts. Do you understand me?''

''Dextro,'' she said automatically. ''Dextro's—''

''No, no; not exactly. We don't know any more about that than you and the others learned last week during Dr Olivant's briefing of scientific personnel.''

''What, then?'' She was dripping and cold, and she had no desire to dress in front of Sixkiller, despite her usual openness about such matters. He was trying to get under her skin. No need, then, to abet him by making herself more vulnerable.

''Time's up for Dr Norn because this was our last day visiting Kyber palaces merely to watch them sleep. Captain Hsi has withdrawn permission for daily field trips.''

Keiko sat down, leaned forward over her tightly

clamped knees, and put her chin in her hands. "That pleases you, I'm sure. Did you engineer the captain's change in policy?"

"I doubt it, Dr Takahashi. If I had that sort of influence, we would have stopped going out there several days before your own first visit to the plain. It's just that Captain Hsi has come to recognize how unprofitable these little expeditions are. The machines are idling. While they idle, Dr Norn is powerless to learn anything significant about them."

"They aren't machines, Farrell."

"They might as well be, hadn't they? Dr Songa has said all along that their behaviour suggests that of an automatic-control system."

"But, Farrell, she still doesn't hold that the Kybers are *nothing* but machines, as you so obsessively do."

"Ah," said Sixkiller, extracting an atomizer from the pocket of a pair of trousers hanging in one of the open lockers, "but Dr Norn is the man with the *true* obsession." He put the atomizer bulb to his nostril and inhaled a whiff of minty-smelling concentrate.

Before she could consider what she was doing Keiko had sprung from the bench and knocked the atomizer out of Sixkiller's hand. "Obsessions come in a variety of packages! You think the Kybers are machines because that's finally what you think people are, isn't it?"

"Is it?" he responded coolly.

"You ascribe to the biological philosophy of Descartes, Farrell. You're a mechanist, a believer in system theory. At every level of analysis, from the molecular right on up, every organism possesses certain control and regulation mechanisms; and if you, Farrell Sixkiller, can get your finger on those, *you* can do the controlling and the regulating. What bothers you about the Kybers is not that they're machines—because they're not, and you know it—but that you can't begin to find the mechanisms of their control!''

"I'm hardly alone in that failure, am I?"

"Perhaps you're alone in wanting to manipulate them, and to manipulate me and anyone else who doesn't share your convictions!''

"Mr Sixkiller!" That was Captain Hsi. His voice echoed in the dome of the bathhouse and reverberated down the corridor to the dressing chamber.

The floater pilot knelt, picked up the fallen atomizer, and returned it to the pocket of his wrinkled trousers. "Coming, sir!" Then he looked at Keiko with annoyingly compassionate eyes. "That which manipulates is alive, Dr Takahashi, and that which suffers manipulation lacks life to the degree that it's controlled."

"Neat. Very neat."

"You're more alive than most, except maybe in your relationship with Dr Norn. As for the Kybers, they're dead, Dr Takahashi, and I'm scared as hell of whatever it is that winds them up, or pulls their wires, or sends juice coursing through their circuits. Scared as hell."

"Mr Sixkiller!"

"Dr Songa says I'm a vitalist, not a mechanist," Farrell Sixkiller continued. "That's what I think, too. I'm glad that our time here is nearly up. Human beings have no business kowtowing to machines, even if they're engineered from DNA—nor any business waiting for the death of a system in which they were first set running."

"Our time here is nearly up?"

"That's right. The *Heavenbridge* received a message from Expeditionary Command yesterday. We're to leave Onogoro—the entire Gemini system—no later than a week after decoupling. Outfitting interstellar expeditions is an expensive business. The bigwigs at

Luna Port aren't going to risk losing a light-skimmer and four dozen highly qualified personnel to an untimely nova, Keiko.''

There. Her first name, as if Sixkiller had decided that in dispensing privileged information he could afford a patronizing intimacy. Keiko recoiled from this presumption, and from the information occasioning it.

"But Craig said we'd have two months' notice, at least. The nova may not occur for another four or five years.''

"Expeditionary Command says we have too little experience of such celestial events to try to soothsay 'em. Despite the expertise of Doctors Olivant and Mahindra, we could still conceivably get fried along with the Kybers. So as soon as we've observed the decoupling, we're to abandon the Platform and head for home with our bodies and souls intact.''

"Mr Sixkiller!"

Keiko turned her back on the floater pilot, stripped her towel aside, and began dressing at her locker. "How long do we have?''

"Fourteen, fifteen days.''

"Does Andrik know this? Does he know you're not going to permit him to go out to the Kyber palaces again?''

"It's not me who isn't permitting him, it's Captain Hsi.''

"All right. Whatever. Does Andrik know?'' She was already reaching for the pulse blower on her locker's top shelf.

"Sure. I thought he ought to know.''

Holding the drier like a weapon, Keiko faced Sixkiller. "And?''

"Captain Hsi probably wants me to pumice his back. If I don't do it now, Lady Keiko, it won't get done. Our time's nearly up, you know.'' He inclined his head, popped the heels of his flip-flops together, and smiled at her with something like pity. Then he left.

"*Mr Sixkiller!*" The echo of the captain's voice had the laughable poignancy of a broken trumpet playing taps.

TWELVE

Necessarily given over to the dog work of consolidating scientific gains and preparing to decamp, the next twelve days passed in a flurry of research activity, shuttle runs, and backbreaking manual labour in the ever-increasing cold.

Maintenance equipment broke down, as did cranes and mobile lifts, with the result that even scientific personnel occasionally found themselves performing such tasks as disassembling nonvital structures and stacking cargo. The Platform was stripped to a functional skeleton of its former self, only the inflatables comprising its lab complex and its essential sleeping quarters going untouched. In fact, before she had a chance to assess her reaction to this frenzied withdrawal, three quarters of Keiko's personal gear—including her microfiche projector and her portfolio of projectable memories—had been packed and shuttled aloft to the *Heavenbridge*.

She was glad to be going home—of that she was not in doubt—but that their sudden decampment might be owing in part to Sixkiller's poisoning of Captain Hsi's attitude toward the Kybers seemed to her an insidious possibility. What if the captain had told Expeditionary Command that the aliens represented a threat to the psychological well-being of humanity? What if, contaminated by his lover's superstitious fear of the Kybers, Captain Hsi had actually *recommended* an early departure from the Gemini system? The impending nova of Dextro would provide a reason for retreat more palatable to human sensibilities—for the fear of a demonstrable danger implied discretion, whereas fear of an unprobed unknown might well be construed as cowardice. No one disputed that Dextro was going to explode, after all, and the only truly controversial aspect of Olivant and Mahindra's prophecy was *when*.

Keiko, caught up in the dismantling of the Platform, mulled these suspicions helplessly, afraid that the dwindling time remaining to the Onogoro Expedition was directly traceable to the subtle influence of Farrell Sixkiller on a man whose professional judgment and integrity she had rarely questioned, even if she no longer found admirable either his off-duty personality or his taste in friends and confidants. It now seemed to Keiko that the captain and the floater pilot had set themselves up in opposition to the pursuit of truth.

But perhaps these suspicions all stemmed from private disappointment, Keiko reflected; perhaps she was being unduly censorious. It was unlike her to engage in the mental gymnastics of paranoia and blame-shifting; and when you carefully considered the matter, you could scarcely fault Expeditionary Command for refusing to play guessing games with the radiative dynamics of a sun and the lives of nearly fifty people. Even if neither Captain Hsi's nor Sixkiller's motives were *entirely* pure, they were not evil men, not cowards, not fools. Why, during this period of logistical upheaval and horrifyingly discoloured skies, had she aligned herself so implacably against the one's leadership and the other's fear-tainted philosophy?

The answer, of course, was Andrik. Embittered by what he viewed as an arbitrary form of house arrest, he had infected her with these very suspicions over the last several days. Although he seldom spoke, holding himself aloof from her under the pretext of collating data from his previous studies of the Kybers, on one recent occasion he had spent an entire work day with her helping to assemble the archives of the knowledge centre for shuttle shipment to the *Heavenbridge*. The window-lens of the inflatable had provided, as always, a chilling panorama of the Onogorovan landscape: a silvered expanse of crater mouths and great, blisterlike boulders. The face of the sun, shimmering alternately red and orange, was pocked with leprous plagues. Meanwhile, the mists streaming from the mountain flanks and migrating like ghost glaciers from the foothills to within only a few kilometres of the Platform twinkled with snapping networks of ice. It was not hard for Keiko to imagine a snowfall at this crucial time drifting to such depth that the legs of the Expeditionary Platform utterly disappeared, stranding them atop the buildup like a raft on an ocean of unbroken white.

As he worked, Andrik kept looking out the window-lens—not at the snows of Keiko's fancy, but at a beckoning terrain of mysteries and wonders forbidden his footprint by a stupid executive decree. The tautness of his face as he disconnected the knowledge centre's computer link to the *Heavenbridge* and unplugged a series of secondary terminals was as expressive of his frustration and anger as any verbal outburst, and Keiko's heart ached with a mute compassion. More out of respect for his pain than from any childish desire to force his hand, she had resolved not to speak intimately until Andrik showed he was ready. Their conversation, then, was limited for long periods to exchanges like "Hand me that microfiche file, would you?" and "Here it is, Kei." That they had once been lovers— had, in fact, fairly recently professed themselves each other's loved one—only a clairvoyant would have been able to perceive.

Finally, nearly two hours after they had taken lunch together in the lecture room of the observatory (for the refectory had already been collapsed and packed away with the bathhouse dome and the skins of several storage balloons), Andrik folded the last of the knowledge centre's study chairs and slid it into the streamlined cargo cart especially made for them.

"Kei," he said, sitting down on the cart and dropping his hands between his knees.

"Yes?"

"Keiko, I'm sorry that I've been the way I have."

She cocked her head. "How have you been?"

"Fine," he responded. "How have *you* been?"

As fragile and uninspired as it so obviously was, this bit of nonsense marked Andrik's first attempt at humour since the day that Craig Olivant had told them that Dextro was going to flare up. Keiko laughed, and Andrik let his lips approximate a smile. The fire had not gone out of him of late; he had simply put it under a bushel and fanned its coals in secret. The smoke from the flames of his personality was bitter, flavoured with wormwood.

"I haven't been able to think about anything but the Kybers."

"I know," she said.

"Listen, Kei. What we're abandoning on Onogoro is more important than either you or me, more important than Sixkiller or the captain or anyone else connected with this expedition.''

A small hostility moved in her. "Why?"

"Because the Kybers have struck through the mask of our illusory reality to what's truly real—"

"Now you sound very much like a Buddhist, Andrik.''

"That shouldn't disturb you, should it? What I'm trying to say is that if Captain Hsi doesn't permit the Kybers to school us in their techniques for achieving a similiar breakthrough, he'll be depriving our entire species of its finest chance for the fulfillment of . . . well, of our spiritual potential.''

"Captain Hsi? By himself? And are you worried about the whole of humanity as much as you are about the individual soul of Andrik Norn?''

"Of course I'm worried about the individual soul of Andrik Norn!'' He squinted at her appraisingly, then got up and strode to the window-lens. "But just as we expeditionary personnel are representatives of everyone who stayed at home, I'm a stand-in for those same people in our dealings with the Kybers. I want what we all should want, Keiko. To deny me in this is to deny multitudes.''

She flushed in acute embarrassment—for him. Did he really have any idea what he had just said?

"A sentiment worthy of any god-king or Stalin, Andrik.''

He winced as if she had slapped him. "Or to deny *you,*" he said in a tone of deliberate reasonableness, comprehending the source of her annoyance. "Or to deny Betti Songa, or Naomi Davis or even Farrell Sixkiller—if, as an adolescent punk in some sagebrush American pesthole, Sixkiller hadn't long ago disqualified himself from that pursuit. It's bad for all of us,

Kei, this stance of the captain's. It's too bad for all of us.''

She approached Andrik and took his hands. Carts were going by on the Platform's decking, and a pair of well-bundled mechanics were painstakingly dismantling a tracking antenna mounted high on an adjacent globe of the observatory. But for the quick-silver mists, the colour of the sky, and the regular spacing of the Kyber palaces on the plain, she might have been gazing down on an uninhabited region of the Moon. Keiko nodded at the landscape, squeezed her lover's fingers.

''You've forgotten something, haven't you?''

''What?''

''That the Kybers haven't co-operated in this. To date, they've done nothing at all to 'school us in their techniques' for obtaining nirvana, if that's where you really believe they are.''

''Somewhere like.'' He pulled one hand free of her grasp and tapped on the curve of the window-lens. ''And you've forgotten something, too, Kei. That your former student invited us to a decoupling ceremony— the Rite of Conjoining, it called that little get-together.''

A dread apprehension gripped Keiko's heart, squeezing it as she had just squeezed her lover's hand. ''We'll be abandoning the Platform then, Andrik. If you were to go out there without permission—''

''Shhhh.'' He was smiling.

She turned away from him. ''I didn't hear what you just said, Andrik. If it finally comes to an open declaration of allegiances, I never heard you say that. I think, too, that I resent your telling me.''

''Don't you want to come?''

''No,'' she said. ''Not against explicit orders to the contrary.''

"Then come to my dormicle tonight. We'll be collapsing all but a few of the sleeping balloons tomorrow and the day following, and privacy—well, there won't be any, Keiko, not until we're back aboard the *Heavenbridge*. More than likely, we'll all be sacking out on the floor of Craig's lecture room. Everybody, that is, except the captain and a few of his favoured cronies."

"Sixkiller among them?"

"Bingo," said Andrik, winking in a sly parody of lechery.

She could not laugh. The invitation that he had just tendered her struck her as a formality; it seemed to promise farewell at least as much as passion, and she thought again of their last full night together, when Andrik's lovemaking had suggested to her what it might be like to be ravaged by a Kyber. The irony of this analogy, of course, lay in the fact that the foremost victim of alien rape on Onogoro was Andrik Norn himself . . .

Meanwhile, Dextro was in the throes of fever; the Kybers were comatose; and the expedition was winding down. As the Kyber planet swung outward along its ellipse toward an inescapable leavetaking, perhaps it was also fitting that she and Andrik should commemorate in each other's arms the disintegration of their love. Ah, that hurt—the very thought hurt, it tore and chafed.

But in the end, for herself as well as for Andrik, she went to his dormicle to suffer the sweet indignity of his caresses.

THIRTEEN

She awoke in the night disturbed by absence, by a disconcerting hollow of cool air.

"Andrik?"

He was gone. From her. From his dormicle.

Already? By night? The defection stung. She felt that she had been left lying in his sheets like a dummy bedroll in the bunk of some prisoner, a ruse to distract the guards while he escaped. She had been lured to his bed for no other reason! Yes, that stung . . . and yet she had told him not to implicate her in his folly and he had given him his promise—tacitly, if no other way. Wasn't that promise printed in her flesh tonight? Or did Andrik imagine that leaving little homunculi of spermatozoa, DNA images of himself, flailing pointlessly inside her cleared him of the blame of abandoning her? Were they and her memories suitable stand-ins for his fleshly warmth?

Naked she rose, careless tonight of the trickle of his seed—his alibi—and roamed his stripped dormicle. She flashed on the sun-bulb and stood blinking against its glare. Was there to be a farewell letter atop her clothes or a final message scribbled on the wall? Had he stylized his departure to such a degree?

But perhaps it was she who was stylizing his departure—by fantasizing about some final letter to mute the pain and the betrayal, to cauterize these. Damn it, I'm still trying to cast him in some noble, dramatic role! *That*, I shall not do.

Swiftly she dressed, and left the dormicle.

A light showed. She hesitated, then hurried on fluttering mothlike toward its flame.

It was Craig Olivant who sat, alone, in the denuded observatory—with a Go board arrayed before him. Loops of white stones ellipsed around black strongholds in no pattern that she had ever seen before.

The astrophysicist looked up. "Ah, the originator of this naughty game! You know, I'm dog-tired, but it seems such a damn shame to sleep. You, too?"

His index finger curved around the pattern of the stones as though tracing out some mystic sign of power. The white stones—she realized belatedly—were set out in some approximate map of Onogoro's interchanging orbit, with gravity wells of black stones representing Laevo, Dextro, Il Penseroso, and El Pesado.

She shook her head. "I'm afraid I slept all too well."

After studying the board, he placed another stone.

Looking at his ruddy face, she was forcibly reminded of another beefy countenance—of a *gaijin* in Kyoto in the winter, long ago, when the arrows had flown time and again. Now, if she chose to, she could speak to him. Now she could speak to genuine aliens, too—but only, still, in human language.

"Occasionally I'm a bit clumsy," he said, touching the board as though trying to find a way to touch on her own problem. He tapped a black stone. "I'm not always the most *dextrous* of people." He looked up at her. "But I've noticed, if I place a stone exactly on each of the cross hairs all the way across the board, they never quite fit into line. I never produce a perfect symmetry."

He was being more evasively allusive than the most discreet Japanese—so much so, in fact, that she was unable to tell whether he was alluding to her problems or his own. Was he simply worried about his own computer-verified calculations of orbits, or about the private orbits of some of his fellow expedition members?

She perched on a stool. "The best boards are designed that way," she said brightly. "And the best stones. The stones are just slightly too large, or else the board is just slightly too small. It's traditional."

He shrugged at the perversity of it, then nodded thoughtfully. "An inherent instability? Like Onogoro's orbit? The stones jostle . . . You know, you'd have to move off the board, on to a meta-board— a meta-cosmos—to get everything absolutely neat. Neat, yeah, and maybe sterile, too. Awful, even? Why am I sitting here like a child playing with pebbles when I've got computers to run through all the billion vectors for me?"

Keiko felt a surge of sympathy for the astrophysicist, who was not quite sure *how* the Moebius tightrope of Onogoro's orbit had come into being, even though he now knew why it worked. Or thought he did.

There was something almost sacramental, she fancied, about what Craig was doing with this Go board: not playing a genuine game with himself—as though between independent brains in the same skull—nor even mapping out true orbits, but rather telling the beads of the universe.

"But it *is* a cosmic game," she said, leaning over,

pointing here, here, there. "Originally, that is. In conception. The nine spots on the board stand for the celestial bodies. And, yes, look," lifting one black stone, "you've got Dextro on one of the special spots, and Laevo down here on another . . ." Can I help him, she wondered, even though I cannot help myself?

Craig Olivant chuckled. "I didn't realize." His clasped blond hair was—well, an accidental pigtail.

She gazed at the very centre of the board, the central spot. She tapped it with her fingernail. "This one is called *taikyoku*, which means something like the Primordial Principle of the Universe."

She did not need to lift a stone. That space was empty. Nothing occupied it. Only absence.

Craig picked up a white stone. His hand dithered, but did not descend. Not yet.

"It's considered to be in bad taste," she murmured, "and inappropriate, to place a stone in the *taikyoku* position in the early stages of the game."

"This game's well advanced," said Craig. "Insofar as this medley can be called a game. Let the Primordial Principle make itself felt! Andrik would like to play this stone, wouldn't he?" he added casually, without looking her in the eye, whereupon he slapped the white stone down.

It was not the same as slipping a final jiwsaw piece into place, thereby locking everything together. The *taikyoku* stone jerked its neighbours aside. A quick shockwave ran along one line of stones. A black stone slid off the edge of the board, into oblivion, into the astrophysicist's maybe meta-space . . .

Keiko wondered if she should tell Craig what was happening. That would not make her responsible for betraying her lover, would it, as he had betrayed her?

Instead she asked, "How could he possibly play that stone?"

A footfall sounded in the corridor.

Jerking erect, bumping the board, she sent stones flying: all Craig's orbits clattered into chaos.

It was Andrik.

"Counselling session?" he asked lightly.

She shook her head. "Where have you been? Where did you go?"

Andrik stared at the shattered binary code of stones, on the table, on the floor. "Not yet," he said vaguely. "I went for a bath."

"In the middle of the night? In this—this *darkness?*" What stain were you hoping to cleanse? she thought. The stain of me? But it is I who am stained . . . She felt the dry pull of the glaze of his seed on her skin. Confused, she bent to gather up the spilt stones, hoping to restore some small sense of order to the night.

"It was like a sensory deprivation tank tonight," came Andrik's voice. "Except that I was afloat in water instead of Epsom salts. The tank was one of the preparatory methods we tried out, you know, at the Xenology Centre in Zurich—as a way of reprogramming ourselves for new alien realities. Simulations of them, anyway. Our guesses, our models." He laughed, a brief, estranging bark. "The ultimate total-immersion experience—except for the nostrils. Complete cut-off of our terrestrial senses. A womb without a view, save an inward one. The amazing thing is that I always felt like I was on fire, even in those calm spaces—my mind burning in the darkness."

Then his hands were drawing her up from the floor. He took the stones from her and tossed them carelessly on the board, as though paying Craig Olivant for the counsel he had not given. Keiko allowed herself to be led from the room, but in the corridor pulled away from Andrik and studied his strange, untroubled face.

"I'm going back to my own dormicle," she said. "I'll neither help nor hinder you, Andrik. Do you understand?"

He nodded. "For that I thank you, Lady Kei." He took her hand again and touched his lips to it in a courtly gesture that seemed to her expressive of genuine emotion. He was bidding her a quiet farewell, not mocking her innocence and confusion.

"Goodbye," she said. Goodbye, not goodnight. She would probably see him again the next day, and even the day after that, for he would not leave until it was too late to turn back—but this moment, this very moment, was goodbye.

"*Sayonara*," he said. He pronounced the word wrong.

FOURTEEN

Precisely when Olivant and Mahindra had predicted its decoupling, seventy-seven days after the arrival of the *Heavenbridge* in synchronous orbit, Onogoro sailed free of Dextro. A stone flung from an immense, centrifugal sling, it flew through the shockwave barrier where the solar wind from its fevered sun collided with the wind from Laevo. The snow that had drifted down on previous days—like powdered sugar buffeted by weird gravitational turbulences, no longer white but iridescent, multicoloured with the wintry spectra of both haloed suns—lay no deeper than a coverlet of silk on the rocks beneath the Platform. Meanwhile, like running paint, auroras dripped down the sky. To Keiko it seemed that the heavens were already melting in nova-light.

It was the evening of the last day.

"Beautiful and spooky," said Craig Olivant, who stood with Keiko, Betti Songa, Naomi Davis, and the atmospheric specialist Nikolai Taras at the western railing of the Platform—just as he had stood with a somewhat differently constituted group on the night that he had used Il Penseroso as a "visual aid" to explain the mechanics of this very decoupling.

Betti shuddered, not merely from the cold. "I can't help thinking that the planet's going to stop turning and throw us out into deep space, the way you go over a bicycle's handlebars when you brake too quickly."

"Well, we haven't braked, have we? Gravity's brakes are off. We're the runaway."

"Lord," said Taras, "I hope they're getting this aboard the *Heavenbridge*: transmission images, atmospheric readings, all the telemetry." Rainbows of colour washed across Taras's face. When he turned, his irises and pupils brilliantly reflected the sky's prismatic light-show. "I suppose I'd better get back to the monitors. It's damn unfair, having to go inside. When am I ever going to witness—with my own naked eyes—an event like this?"

"Stop grumbling," Craig advised him. "You've been out here plenty. Besides, I'm taking mental photographs for you."

Taras raised his hand in mock anger, as if to cuff the astrophysicist, then shuffled off toward the observatory, all the while rubbernecking the heavens.

The globes of the observatory and that of the single remaining inflataform shone white and orange and indigo, like soap bubbles turning under coloured lamps. On the southeastern corner of the Platform stood the final shuttle from the light-skimmer, poised for a midnight departure, a spire with polarized slit-windows girdling its fuselage like the cartridge chambers of an old-fashioned pistol . . .

As Taras entered the observatory, another figure

jostled him briefly in the opening, then rebounded and swaggered toward the railing. It was Captain Hsi, out, it seemed, strolling the deck of his planetside command in a kind of sentimental farewell observance.

Except that Keiko knew exactly what was brewing, had expected the matter to climax hours ago, and wished that she could avoid this confrontation, just as she had earlier managed to sidestep a minor administrative meeting with the captain and two communal meal periods.

"Good evening," said the captain when he had joined them, observing the amenities and prolonging Keiko's agony.

The group murmured a number of indistinguishable responses, overridden by Naomi's pointedly demanding, "So we *are* going to leave them to their fate, eh? No reprieve for the Kybers and no guilty consciences for leaving them in the frying pan? If we ever *do* come back, you know, they'll be about as communicative as a plate of burnt kippers."

"My conscience is clear," said Captain Hsi, shivering. His Pekinese eyes bulged with a suppressed rebuke. "Where is Dr Norn?"

This was obstensibly addressed to all four of them, but Keiko took the brunt of the question. The others had clearly not even considered the matter, having occupied themselves, until their spontaneous outing to the rail, with the last-minute details of decamping—so that now they turned to her automatically, as a single person, with the captain's pointed inquiry mirrored in their eyes. Where *was* Dr Norn?

Keiko did not answer. She had no idea what to say.

"Surely you know where your lover is, Dr Takahashi?"

"I'm right here," said Naomi hurriedly, trying to defuse the situation with a joke that conveyed more wistfulness than bite. No one laughed, but Keiko could feel the others' curiosity give way to sympathy and apprehension. Captain Hsi was almost unfailingly polite, even if chilly in his correctness, and that he should descend to innuendo or personal abuse said a great deal about his state of mind, most of it unpleasant. It made Keiko angry.

"Do you kow where Farrell Sixkiller is, sir?"

This retort shocked Betti Songa and Craig Olivant at least as much as it delighted Naomi Davis, but it ricocheted off Captain Hsi like a pebble off a concrete wall. "I repeat, Dr Takahashi: where is Dr Norn?"

She felt her anger and her resolve caving in, toppling into a maelstrom of divided loyalties and repressed self-doubts. She gestured vaguely at the Onogorovan plain and the chaos of auroras above it.

"Out there. Somewhere."

"How long has he been—out there—somewhere—" Each phrase was a razor, slicing away the threadbare fabric of her self-confidence.

"I'm not completely sure. Since two or three hours ago, I believe. I didn't say goodbye to him, and I didn't help him get ready to go."

"But you didn't prevent him, either."

Craig, staring in disbelief at the crater-pocked terrain, dragon-snorted, "What the hell—what the hell is he *doing* out there, anyway?"

"I didn't try to prevent him," Keiko confessed. "Not today, at least."

"We are supposed to leave in approximately five hours, Dr Takahashi. Did you consider that? Nor does the *Heavenbridge* depart this world without its full complement of crew and scientific personnel. That means that you—by your failure to report Dr Norn's intentions to me—have obstructed the purposes and the directives of Expeditionary Command. I hereby relieve you of your duties."

"Which means you won't have to truck crates aboard the shuttle before we take off," Naomi offered by way of sardonic consolation.

"Shut up, Dr Davis!"

"Keiko," said Betti, impulsively embracing her there on the high, flame-lit scaffold, "Keiko, you've not done well. Oh, Kei, how could you let this happen?"

She had no answer. Her eyes on the cold pyrotechnics of decoupling, she accepted the cyberneticist's embrace and patted her consolingly on the hump of her parka. Indeed, Keiko regretted her behaviour more because it stimulated the others' sympathy than because it embodied a private disgrace. Once upon a time, she knew, a Japanese woman in her position would have reached automatically for the knife and readied it at her throat. But, no, she was not going to die for Andrik Norn. Whatever duty toward him she had ever owed was now wholly fulfilled; and, she told herself, in some ways her duty to the expedition was best served not by unthinking surrender to the dictates of a man like Captain Hsi but by rigorous obedience to . . . . well, to what Andrik had once called "hunch and circumstance." Smiling, she put her chin on Betti's shoulder. That was why she had let him go out there, if not also—though it would never do to admit this aloud—for the sake of the Kybers themselves . . .

Captain Hsi glanced back toward the lab complex. "Milius's floater is already aboard the *Heavenbridge*.

Where's the other?''

"There," said Craig, jabbing heavily with his mittened hand. "Beyond the inflatadorm. You can see its nose."

"Dr Norn went out there *on foot?*'' The captain tapped Betti's shoulder and gingerly eased her aside. Face to face with Keiko, he cried, "I've never authorized anyone to venture out there on foot! Never!''

Unable to repress the urge, no matter how incongruous or self-defeating Keiko laughed at the man.

"Oh," said Naomi. "You wish those who disobey you to do it within a framework of obedience. Or vice versa, I suppose.''

"The distinction," said Captain Hsi pedantically, "is that had he taken the floater, we might have expected his immediate safe return. Now that's a doubtful prospect. We must go after him. If he perishes pursuing whatever it is he seeks—'' He looked meaningfully at Keiko.

"Then let me go with you," she said.

"Oh, I insist upon it, Dr Takahashi. I do not relieve you of *that* duty. Moreover, you taught the Kybers—all of them—to speak, and you may prove useful out there." He bowed crisply to each of the people at the railing. "Good night, Dr Olivant, Dr Davis, Dr Songa. Good night.'' Then, gripping Keiko's elbow, he herded her unceremoniously away from her friends, toward the blister of the dormitory. The deck plates under their feet were awash with a flicking tide, and the inflatadorm shimmered beneath the barrage of a dozen bright auroras.

Keiko shook herself free of the captain's grip, to demonstrate that she could walk with him without assistance.

"Mr Sixkiller!" he bellowed distractedly.

"Ah, so you do know where he is."

"We need someone not only to fly the floater, but to take us to the heart of the Kyber maze."

They went together through the hooped archway of the dormitory. Only a few privileged personnel still maintained sleeping quarters here, everyone else having been shunted—exactly as Andrik has predicted—into the lecture room of the observatory. The central corridor of this dorm always suggested to Keiko the ribbed innards of a whale, aglow with a pale blue bioluminescence. Captain Hsi led her through the gloom to the double-unit dormicle that everyone on the Platform knew to be his. The other four units belonged to Sixkiller, Eshleman, Sharon Yablon, and the floater pilot Milius, who had disassembled his craft yesterday and taken it aboard a shuttle. No one had petitioned to occupy his abandoned unit.

"Mr Sixkiller!"

The captain thumbed open his door and entered, pulling Keiko after by her wrist and simultaneously activating the dormicle's sun-bulb. A noise like insects scurrying greeted these preliminaries, and then Keiko, half-blinded by the brilliance of the light, understood that this noise betrayed a frantic shifting of fabrics and linen.

She squinted. A heat-quilt slid aside, and there on the bedstead she saw Clemencia Venáges naked atop the sprawled and supine body of Farrell Sixkiller. The planetologist's back was frozen upright in a lovely curve, and her startled profile revealed one wide liquid eye and a veil of dark, dishevelled hair. Sixkiller's eyes were closed, almost as if in pain. Clemencia's hips concealed, and maybe even contained, a portion of his nakedness.

"We need a floater pilot, Mr. Sixkiller," said Captain Hsi. "We need a floater pilot right now."

"All right," said Sixkiller without opening his eyes.

Clemencia folded her arms across her breasts and blinked through a tangle of hair. "Hello, Kei. Is that you?"

"It's me," she acknowledged. "Hello."

The captain's hand moved to the wall, and he killed the sun-bulb. "These are my quarters. Those who come to my quarters must have a personal invitation, or they must be brought here by me."

"Yes, sir," said Sixkiller and Clemencia together.

Taking advantage of the dark, through which slid faint hints of the turmoil in Onogoro's skies, Clemencia disengaged from the floater pilot and gracefully searched out her clothes. An unhooded window-lens silhouetted her movements. Keiko tried to retreat back into the corridor, but Captain Hsi restrained her, as if honour required no strategic abandonment of one's own nest, no matter how vilely it was polluted or how provocatively besieged.

"For five more hours this dormicle belongs to me," he said. "We are going to a Kyber palace together, Mr Sixkiller, but while we're gone no one is to presume to use my quarters." He ignored Clemencia Venáges, but his tone clearly implied that a randy Clemencia might lead still others to his private nest. Binary love-sharing was one thing, which could be blinked at—but not if it happened in his own sheets. Hsi had just, in a sense, been cuckolded visibly by the pilot, but Hsi obviously preferred to believe it was Clemencia's fault.

"Yes, sir," Sixkiller said dutifully.

Keiko backed away. "I'm going out for a breath of air, Captain Hsi. Please tell me when you're ready to leave.'' This time he made no move to hinder her, and , bemused and fretful, she escaped to the frigid safety of the Platform.

FIFTEEN

The seats in the floater were cold. She could feel their iciness even through the bulk of her thermal clothing. But when Sixkiller activated the blowers set like chromium mouths under the long canopy, the floater filled with warmth so rapidly that Keiko gasped and threw back her hood.

"Let's go," said Captain Hsi.

The lifted off the Platform and swept out over the plain in a soundless arc. Keiko, looking back at the receding tower on which she and the others had lived for seventy-seven days, was plunged into a recollection that had nothing to do—so far as she could determine by occasionally stepping clear of the emotional vise of her reverie—with either Onogoro or the Kybers.

Once, in her girlhood, her parents had taken her with her older brother and sister on a family outing to Tokyo. The Takahashis had gone in the spring, following northwards the triumphal progress of the cherry blossoms, their pink and white clouds billowing upon the land—while the sky itself remained cloudless, a thin, porcelain blue. The cinder cone of Fuji wore a generous ice-cream cap of snow. As they swung past along the tracks at bullet speed, Keiko almost tasted Fuji. Soon, in the city itself, sight and savour, piquant aroma and sound, all crescendoed for her, setting the seal ''Tokyo'' indelibly on the scroll of her memory.

So many sights and sensations! The octopus arms of overhead expressways, aerial bobsled runs humming with turbine-powered taxis and mini-trucks . . . And then the skyscrapers, dripping neon messages so rapidly down their lengths that the buildings appeared to be sinking into the ground and then magically reconstituting themselves in mid-air . . . At the surface of the city proper, such bustle and confusion: shops crowded with pearls, and silks, and Go sets, with tanks of dozing hundred-year-old carp or goggle-eyed ebony goldfish; restaurants where Hokkaido crabs flexed their metre-long arms, dazed by their fall from grace in the northern sea; and fish shops, whose mongers sloshed buckets of ice water over piled-up, gasping shoals, all the while chanting their wares. Clouds of incense drifted from the shrines between the street stalls and bars, the Go parlours and *pachinko* arcades . . . Overhead, flotillas of red and white balloons, cascading neon *kanji* down their guy ropes. Atop one department store, globes of Jupiter and Saturn, their moons swinging about them in an orrery ballet of lights. Atop another such emporium, a full-scale Mississippi steamboat! . . . And beneath the surface, accessible by huge, zipperlike escalators, the crowded fluorescent labyrinths of the undercity.

Nothing in Keiko's previous experience had ever been so vivid. Whatever happened afterward—no matter how sweet, or tart, or bright, or piercing, or terrible—all subsequent experience would overlie the

memory signatures of her trip to Tokyo like plastic
transparencies with no distinct character of their own.
Even at the age of eight, Keiko had understood this.
Although unable to communicate this mystical discovery to her parents, she had let them know that they could
not possibly extend their stay in Tokyo long enough to
satisfy her cravings for its smells, colours, noises,
tastes. Delighted, they had laughed, and she with them,
vibrant as a temple bell.

But on their last day in the city she had behaved
badly, not whining or demanding—but hanging back
with a studied ruthlessness, refusing both food and
drink as if she mistrusted the likely savour of any final
meal in Tokyo. They were on the Ginza, late in the
afternoon, and her parents, ordinarily indulgent to the
point of servility, stiffened their resolve and scolded her
for trying to halt time. She would not be able to accomplish that, they informed her, by dragging the heels
of her new patent-leather shoes. Such behaviour was
not only wicked, in the context of her obligations to
others, but quite pointless.

Here the scolding had ended. Along with her brother
and sister, Keiko was marched into a monstrous department store, quick with customers and clerks, rau-
cous with fishboys in the food hall, discreet with
kimono-clad employees stationed at the foot of each
escalator with a duster for the rubber rail. ''Welcome,
welcome, welcome,'' they intoned, bowing with pup-
pet regularity. The Takahashis rode up. At each floor
they were serenaded by salesgirls reciting their sing-
song inventories: gold-lacquer ware, screens, *cloi-
sonné;* dolls, bridal costumes, coral; restaurants
(French, Indonesian, *sushi, tempura*); microelec-
tronics, imitation extrasolar imports, recent holofiches
of alien landscapes . . .

Finally the Takahashis disembarked together on the margin of a penthouse pavilion given over to the whir-rings and collisions of . . . yes, vintage bump 'em cars. Or maybe they were repro, modern facsimilies. Except in the league table of ''face'' among competing store managers, the distinction scarcely mattered. Electricity crackled under the roof of the pavilion as adults and children charged their squat vehicles around the concrete floor, banging the cars together or whirling them in noisy holding patterns. Keiko, along with sister Etsuko and brother Okido, gawked.

Soon the three of them were wheeling about in the bump'em cars, too. Mother and Father, having de-flected Keiko from her unseemly behaviour, stood at the pavilion rail and with gestures and shouts urged their children to fly around the perimeter of the rink. In their own jerkily advancing car, Keiko looked out on a sea of anonymous foes, all of them, it seemed, intent on driving her smack into somebody else's vehicle, or up against a bumper rail, or maybe even through the pavil-ion's supporting columns and so out into the airspace over the Ginza itself—into the clutches of gravity and death.

A pair of cars bracketed her own, nudging, ricochet-ing, and converging again, whereupon a driver in front of her—a grown man wearing a thin moustache and a navy-blue cravat—abruptly spun his car about so that its blunt nose knocked Keiko's car into the one on her right. Then another car collided with hers. And another. Suddenly every face over every disc-like steer-ing wheel, Okido's and Etsuko's among them, was homing in on her with murderous hilarity flashing in its eyes. Her brother was a vengeful samurai, whirling to the attack. Fearful that this was a punishment secretly planned by Mother and Father, Keiko began to scream

. . . And so her last, and starkest, memory of Tokyo was of the terror she had experienced in the bump'em car pavilion on the uppermost level of that bustling department store on the Ginza.

Bump'em cars, of all things. She imagined a bevy of them spinning about on the deck plates of the Platform, their vertical motive rods extending directly into the auroras discharging their lightning over Onogoro. That image, Keiko realized, somehow tied together the girl she was at eight and the self-doubting person she was today.

Her days under heaven were bridged by joy and regret.

They were over the Kyber palace where Andrik, Betti, and Sixkiller had first found her prize pupil, the crater in which several members of its family had actually condescended to speak to her and Andrik before willing themselves back into kybertrance. The floater banked as if to put down on a nearby ledge, a surface of slate twinkling with diamonds of frost.

"No," said Captain Hsi, who had been talking with Sixkiller about nothing much at all, avoiding the subject of Clemencia's presence in his dormicle and staring pensively at the alien landscape as he spoke. "No, Mr Sixkiller, I want you to hover over the central atrium. Flood it with light. We don't have time to wander through one of those foggy mazes only to discover that our Kybers are all off visiting some other clan, in some other labyrinth."

"They don't do that," Sixkiller said.

"Nevertheless—"

So the floater tilted back toward the centre of the ruins, eased itself into hover, and rotated a few degrees on its long axis so that its passengers could peer down into the pit.

Three thick beams of light picked out the angles of the rocks. These crossed and recrossed, then expanded to illuminate the trapezoidal living chamber. Noonday over an arctic ocean.

Sixkiller dropped them lower and lower, and Keiko feared that the floater would indeed crush the inhabitants of the ruins. For, clearly, the ruins *were* occupied, and Andrik Norn, whom she had tried to send magnanimously on his way and then put completely from her mind, stood foreshortened in the enclosure, his white face washed out in the glare. Around him were grouped five aliens, all in postures of obeisance or prayer, while beyond them, back to back on a long stone bier, lay fused carcasses of the group's pregnant couple. Everything was much as it had been on Keiko's other two trips to the plain, except that tonight the Kybers were animate and her former lover had positioned himself at the centre of a living, five-pointed star. It was impossible to tell what Andrik's expression was or exactly what sort of ritual he was celebrating with the Kybers.

Captain Hsi leaned back in his seat and released a sigh of weary satisfaction. ''Land, Mr Sixkiller.''

The pilot obeyed, carrying them in a swift upward sweep out of the bowl of the labyrinth and then setting them down on a craggy ridge. The legs of the floater touched the gem-bright coverlet of snow almost daintily, then popped with tensile strain as the fuselage settled its weight.

Captain Hsi made no move to undo his seat belt. He stared straight ahead, out through the canopy at the distant Onogorovan mountains, luminous in the ice mists and auroral shadows. Keiko and Sixkiller waited.

Finally the captain said, ''You're to take Dr

Takahashi through the maze, Mr Sixkiller, then escort her back here with Dr Norn.''

"That's all?''

"Do it as quickly as you can.''

"Then there's no need for Dr Takahashi to go,'' said Sixkiller. "You both sit tight, and I'll be back with Dr Norn pronto-presto.''

"I think you had better take Dr Takahashi with you. She has this last duty to fulfil, Mr Sixkiller, and Dr Norn, having deserted us for obsessions of his own, may have very little inclination to obey a summons conveyed through you.''

"All right. If that's how you want it.''

"Leave the blowers on,'' said Captain Hsi.

Before Keiko and Sixkiller could climb down from their seats and exit the floater, however, there reared up beyond its canopy four stilt-walking Kybers. They looked to be half blind. Their forward pupils had shrunk to mere specks in their gleaming, mahogany faces; and their lateral pupils were set too far to the sides of their heads to be readily visible from the floater. They tottered up from the crater like so many remote-controlled machines, then peered blindly through the canopy at the bewildered human beings huddling in its cone of warmth. This was something new. Keiko felt trapped.

"What do they want?'' Captain Hsi asked no one in particular, his calm so steady and reasonable-sounding that it nearly calmed her, too.

"Let the linguist parlay with 'em and maybe we'll find out.'' The floater pilot had his hand on his utility belt, a thumb on the butt of the laser.

Keiko noticed that the cloaks of flesh or quasi-flesh draping the Kybers' arms and torsos were hanging in tatters. The Rite of Conjoining? Was there a link be-

tween their ravaged appearance and that mysterious
rite? Andrik had come out here to participate in that
event, and she feared that he had not been disappointed
in his quest. She was reminded of the strips of skin
flensed from beached porpoises by the peasant peoples
on the coasts near Kushimoto, her mother's birthplace;
of wet parchment; and of tissues grown in versatile ropy
cultures by the transplant technicians of latter-day
Tokyo . . .

"Well, then," she said, "let me go see."

She went down the recessed stairs below her seat,
waited for Sixkiller to spring the door for her, and leapt
out into the night. Tottering, the Kybers gravitated toward her as if she possessed some secret necessary to
their survival. She fell back a step, caught herself, and
stared up at the haloed faces, each of which turned to
scrutinize her with one of its pulsing lateral eye-bulbs.

Thanatoscopes, Andrik had called them: instruments
for perceiving death-in-life and life-in-death.

"We're l-leaving your wor-world," Keiko stam-
mered. "I've come for Dr Norn; he's required to return
with us."

She could not tell if any of the aliens looming above
her now, appraising her with their death-eyes, happened to be the one she had taught—but she doubted
that her former student had abandoned Andrik to greet
their floater and feared that to these Kyber representatives her words were an incomprehensible mish-mash.
Last time out? Well, maybe that had been a dream.

One of them confirmed the reality of both that other
occasion and this: "Lady Keiko, I am to take you
through the labyrinth. These others, your colleagues,
madmen," gesturing at the canopy and its occupants,
"have no invitation. The human supplicant currently at

the heart of our rite, by right of invitation, has asked that we bar them from seeking him out."

"But . . . but I?" she managed.

"He had hoped you were aboard," said the Kyber. "He has told us that your insanity is not so virulent as theirs, those others."

"My *insanity?*"

" 'Persistent mental disorder or derangement'," the Kyber crooned, its voice a mellow piping. "A disruption of process, a failure of control, a crapping-out of steersmanship."

"Andrik Norn said *I* was insane?"

The other three aliens, aloft on their stilts, regarded her with eyes whose front-facing pupils had begun to dilate and glow. One Kyber made a cluck-clucking sound, whereupon they all retreated to take up separate posts around the ticking wasp-shape of the floater.

"Come, Lady Keiko," urged her guide.

SIXTEEN

She followed. This time there were no ghostly blue markings on the walls of the labyrinth; their way was a way of stones, billowing ice mists, darkness. So certain of her docility, or so indifferent to her safety, seemed the creature leading her that it picked its path over the snow-sprinkled flagstones without ever turning its head to note how well or ill she was keeping up.

Keiko, scrupulous to a fault, did not permit herself to lag. By trotting a little, skipping a little, she managed to negotiate every turn—every unexpected doorway inward—without losing sight of the Kyber's bobbing halo-crest.

Suddenly the corridor opened upon the atrium at whose heart stood Andrik and the only other animate member of the alien family. Keiko hesitated, uncertain what to expect of the man who had broken with her, and with all his fellows on the Platform, without ever really renouncing his native allegiances. Indeed, he had come out here on the pretext of discovering from the Kybers a means whereby humanity could slip its biological and philosophical fetters and attain a sort of perfect awareness available to the Kybers in death-sleep. How that grandiose goal contrasted with the bleak and dismaying reality of these surroundings!

His parka hood thrown back and his coat unzipped to his breastbone, Andrik turned to face her with glittering eyes.

"Kei!" he said, rushing forward to embrace her. For a moment his cheek was hot against hers; then he drew back and peered at her with what seemed grateful wonder, unmindful of the cold, the fiery skies, the tomblike resonances of the Kyber pit. "You've come," he murmured. "They allowed you to come."

"Because they want you to come back," Keiko replied. "Captain Hsi and Sixkiller are waiting—" She tried to indicate the ridge, but Andrik clapped his hands to her arms and pulled her with him toward the waiting Kyber. Their boots crunched across a glaze of snow reflecting the incessant auroral streaming overhead.

"This is Alice," said Andrik, nodding at the creature. "I call it Alice. I call the one behind you Alice, too. In fact, I call them all Alice—but *this* Alice is the one who skipped from its side of the looking glass to ours long enough to learn our lingo."

"Yes, I knew—"

"Keiko Takahashi, Alice. Alice, Keiko." He spoke deferentially to the alien: "You also knew, of course. These are just formalities, a bit of small talk before her initiation."

"What initiation, Andrik?" She wanted to rezip his parka to his Adam's apple and pull its hood back over his head where it belonged—annoying maternal stirrings that did not altogether obscure the uneasiness welling in her. *What initiation?*

"Like Alice, they grow and shrink and grow again at will. But that's only out here, up here, where we can see

them." Andrik shook his raw, mittenless hands at
shoulder height, indicating the Kyber world chillily
ablaze about them. "But down the rabbit hole of consciousness, down there, deep inside, where it's hell for
us to follow—and heaven, too—they're not very much
like that little-girl-tourist Alice at all; they're more like
Mad Hatters, March Hares, and Cheshire Cats—native
to the place. Permanent residents. To tell the truth, I
don't really know what we ought to call them when
they're down there. It's we who are the Alices when we
try to follow, we who are susceptible to—"

His gabbiness, his excitement, panicked her. "Andrik!" she cried, clutching at his sleeve and turning
him. "Andrik, you're babbling!"

"Then perhaps you're not listening," said the Kyber
to whom Andrik had led her; her former student, Alice.

"We're leaving Onogoro," Keiko told the alien.
"I've got to take him back to the floater. Our departure
is only—"

Alice knelt gracefully just to Keiko's left. Then it
extended toward her one of its mailed fists. Like a crane
in shallow water, the other Kyber approached. It inter-
posed itself between Andrik and Keiko on her right, but
neither knelt nor offered her its hand. Andrik went
penitentially to his knees. Behind him lay the Kybers
bound back to back in their disquieting death-sleep
pregnancy.

"Take Alice's hand," he urged her.

"Why?" She recoiled from the Kyber, from the
quirky nuances of this ceremony. She did not want to
put her knees to the cold, snow-layered rock, or to
commit herself as deeply as had Andrik to an idealism
that neither of them could confirm the truth of without
alien assistance. *He* was insane, not she or Captain Hsi
or the truculent Farrell Sixkiller, and now he was trying

to exploit her for the purposes of that singleminded insanity.

"To see what the Kybers see," he said.

"They're going to die, Andrik. Their sun is going to blaze up, and they're going to die. Or they'll die during transit—as Onogoro limps through this ungodly winter toward the hearth they hope to find in Laevo."

"It's a most *godly* winter, Lady Keiko. That hearth is also a haven, processor of our dreams and seed."

This was from the standing Kyber, her guide, who peeled a strip of quasi-flesh from the drape of its right arm and offered it to her with easy dignity.

"Eat thou this in remembrance of what thou hast never been," it said in exact repeat of her former student's command to Sixkiller, how many days ago . . .?

"I've . . . I've tasted kyberflesh," said Keiko, demurring.

"You found it bitter?" her guide asked.

"Very bitter. Unpalatable. I can't."

"You didn't give it a chance, Kei. I've eaten of it, too, several times—in order to get where they go naturally in death-sleep. The initial bitterness fades. Don't spurn Alice's invitation to . . . to heaven!"

"But you're *different*, Andrik, having eaten of it."

"Of course I'm different!" he declared impatiently. "What would be the point of eating kyberflesh merely for its savour? This isn't cannibalism or predation, it's holy communion!"

"Eat thou this," her guide warbled again.

"No, I can't."

"For me, then," pleaded Andrik. "I love you, Keiko, and not so very long ago you said that you loved me."

"For you?" Keiko stared bemusedly at Andrik,

kneeling before her in the snow like the humbled Emperor Somebody in sackcloth at the gates of Rome. "By taking part in this freakish communion, you want me to *prove* my love for you?" Taunted by some archaic social parallel that would not come wholly clear, she smiled her disappointment and perplexity.

"I want you to let me give you this gift, Kei. It's not a proof of love, it's mutual expression of it."

She was moved by these words, by the way Andrik looked while saying them. She turned to her guide and hesitantly accepted the strip of flesh, wondering as she did so if she were simply succumbing to Andrik's glibness. The flesh was greasy with the vinegary exudation long since familiar to her, even though the last piece of kyberflesh she had tasted had been as dry as impacted ashes.

"Eat me," said the alien, parodying the instruction labels in Wonderland. "Eat me, Lady Keiko."

Andrik's face was beatific in the angry heaven-glow. Go on, it prompted her; taste of Alice that you may share with me an imitation of the state called kybertrance. His face—his eyes—persuaded her, and she fed herself the icy Onogorovan jerky in tiny twists that briefly gummed her crowns before melting on her palate and sliding down her throat. One Alice loomed while another Alice knelt, and Andrik was a fresh-faced boy between them.

The initial bitterness of the kyberflesh gave way to a taste like mandarin oranges marinated in sweet French brandy. Soon, tipsy with strangeness, she was gripping the mailed fingers of Alice A and Alice B and sinking to her knees opposite the man whose love had led her to this pass. To the Kyber Pass . . ., she thought ridiculously. The Kybers' heads moved from side to side in purposeful rhythm, as if trying to fix her stereoscopically with their meta-eyes. Then the nodding slowed, and their lights went out, like pinball games on which the plugs have been abruptly pulled.

They were "dead," deep in kybertrance, avatars of the divine couple of Japanese myth, Izanagi and Izanami. They were alien-gods cut adrift in a mythic realm dredged from Keiko's own subconscious yet galvanized by lightning bolts of statement and demand from Somewhere Else . . .

SEVENTEEN

Was the streaming chaos overhead really the sky or merely a series of phantom images projected on the screens of her inner vision? Why had she not frozen to death? Perhaps she had. Or perhaps there drifted through her blood a glycol antifreeze distilled from what she had already reluctantly eaten of the Kyber.

This place that she, and they, inhabited was a place between Heaven and Hell, a limbo of uncertain possibilities. A noise like the lurching of bump'em cars punctuated the silence of which it was apparently woven: a humming silence connected to that ineffable Somewhere Else still just beyond her grasp.

Nevertheless, energies and auras, the currency of death-in-life, flowed between her and the others in their little diamond of external touching; and she saw in death-sleep a flicker of lightning against the tarnished mother-of-pearl of her inward sky: **Do you feel pain, Lady Keiko?** This was from her former student, Alice A, no longer its family's septa-prime. And, yes, almost coinciding with its question, she had experi-

enced an ache or a hunger for which she could imagine
no effective balm or nourishment.

That's good, hummed Alice A, even though she
had framed no response either silently or aloud, for a
little of that mysterious pain nagged her yet. **Pain
is the First Mover, Lady Keiko, at whose touch we
flee the stagnation of complacency and self-
righteousness.**

And pleasure is the reward of escape, sang
Alice B in kybertrance. **Moving from pain to pleasure, we grow.**

If the pain *is* escapable, Keiko cautioned the
aliens in her own cold approximation of death-sleep,
trying to locate Andrik in the grey recesses of its
sky—whereupon her mind hung Dextro there, a lamp
about to gutter. How escapable was the pain heralded
by that image . . .?

**Perhaps the greatest boon of intelligence is that it
permits the vivid anticipation of otherwise abstract
pain,** crooned Alice A. **Evil and entropy are avatars of pain, and therefore as necessary to an evolving
datum state as the pleasure that rewards successful
evolution.**

None of this made sense to Keiko, not even in her
quasi-kybertrance. She wanted out. She wanted to
break her psychic bonds with Izanagi and Izanami—no,
with Alice A and Alice B. She wanted to recall her mad
lover to normal consciousness and return with him
aboard the *Heavenbridge* to Earth. That escape would
indeed be a pleasure, and she struggled against the
lightning flashes pinioning her where she knelt . . . It
seemed the Rite of Conjoining was less a sharing of
bodily warmth—a quality that the Kybers held in no
particular esteem—than an activator of continent-wide
data exchange. Regardless of her desires and doubts,

she was interwired with her Alices and maybe even beyond them to other death-sleeping Onogorovans. Struggle was pointless.

Where, then, was Andrik? Treading psychic water with the aliens' indeterminate God-Behind-the-Galaxies . . .?

We are evolving in response to an anticipated pain, vouchsafed one or both of the Kybers. **We are evolving at the behest of our own intelligence but in response to our intelligent perception of a control system *greater* than Kyber self-awareness. This control system is our God.**

Is it Andrik's, too?

Tied end to end, the neuronic axons of the human brain—if the cerebral makeup of your lover is typical of the species—would stretch one and a quarter million kilometres. That is the length of the unitary human mind, Lady Keiko; and as great as that may seem to you, as 'rapidly' as the synapses along that involute network do spark and fire, it may yet be insufficient to apprise itself of the God manifest within us as a programme for our own survival.

Now Keiko was lost not only in the fog of death-sleep but in the briary thickets of Kyber metaphysics. Her eyes were open—her physical eyes—but all she could see, now that her initial pain and fear had subsided, was a kind of photographic negative of the aurora-riven night. No way back, no way forward; no way out.

Unitary brain? protested Andrik's consciousness from the depths of the aliens' all-encompassing trance. **What do you mean? Ours is a double brain— left hemisphere, right hemisphere, a membranous bridge between. That's how we're communicating now, isn't it?**

Not entirely, fluted Alice A, with irony.

In fact, amended Andrik's disembodied voice, **it's really a *triple* brain! Cortex, limbic system, brainstem—higher thought, animal passion, automatic housekeeping.**

Our apologies, O complex being—but the tripartite human brain operates, we find, at a single speed.

Andrik acquiesced in this judgment, or else the psychic give-and-take of kybertrance dovetailed gradually into silence, like a radio station fading away into static as its listeners physically outrun it.

Tilting her head back, Keiko stared with blind eyes at the heavens. Human beings had no lateral eye-bulbs, no bodily means of perceiving metaphysical reality, and this gauzy limbo between two realms began again to spook and weaken her.

What were the aliens seeing? Archangels trumpeting resurrection? The light beyond the final curvature of space? The face of God? Projecting herself into a blind spot that was perhaps for the Kybers a lens on supranormal events, Keiko tried to break through to them. Her "voice" was mottled with psychic static:

Perhaps I see, she told the silence. **Your brains must work at different speeds. A faster speed when you're 'living', walking about as human beings walk, and a slower, more thoughtful speed when you're interwired with one another in death-sleep.**

The other way round, Lady Keiko. The other way round. Consider. (This was Alice A, her student, piping its message across the murmuring darkness in which she feared they had abandoned her.) **Kybernetically speaking, not to steer you wrong, a control system—axiomatically, I remind you—is always faster than the process which it controls. It packs more data. Data-packed, it embodies a vaster wisdom and a more protean, if ultimately immortal, spirit. The system governing a galaxy, Lady Kei, must have a wave-period far faster than that of any of the constituent or participatory elements of the galaxy under goverance.**

I don't—

Neither did Andrik, but he is beginning to. Thus, being faster than, it is also invisible to, those constituent or participatory elements. If they could actually perceive it, it would not be the system of goverance to which I am alluding. *Ipso facto*.

Since the system can't be seen, Keiko hazarded, **it therefore exists.**

Koan du jour! exclaimed the Kyber. **It is all a question of tempo. Flesh-life unravels its organic processes too slowly to integrate meaningfully with its control.**

But how can you prate about tempo, you whose tempo is virtually nil more often than not? Even now we're trapped in a little death, slaves of stasis . . .

And yet she had a dim understanding that mailed fists gripped her hands, and that her fingers inside her frozen gloves were still capable of movement and sensation. In fact, her perception of an incomplete numbness was proof that she had not ''died'' as wholeheartedly as had the Kybers. She could still move and feel, even as if through several layers of surgical dressings or mummy-cloth. The stasis to which she had just claimed to be enslaved was in her case highly imperfect and therefore highly promising, a womb rather than a tomb. . . .

By and large, in the warmth of perihelion, Lady Keiko, we follow the path of flesh and think flesh-brain thoughts—

But at aphelion, when your world is furthest from the sun, you commit yourselves more frequently to kybertrance, and to whatever that implies?

True, O little teacher. We are quite flexible in our design. We have great localized control over our body temperatures. When you first arrived—I mean, of course, you and all your cohorts from the *Heavenbridge*—it was essential that we formulate a flesh-life response in order to acquire more data. One must dance a bit to keep the circulation going, and I was the principal dancer through whose pauses my peers and subscribers partook of the data I did dance for.

In kybertrance you gave your people the gift of human language?

Human language is merely one variety of data. Lady Keiko; I gave my people the gift of data. But we knew that this was an unusual year, made more unusual still by the ostensibly secular advent of humankind. We knew that this was the leap-year of our interstellar winter. We delayed as long as possible the universal hyber-preservation from which several of your party have lately sought to rouse us, only you and this persistent other succeeding—by virtue, I declare, of our approving that success. Eventually it seemed to all of us together that the Control System mediating our lives between illusion and meta-illusion desired our aid in conveying to you the Gospel According to Kybertrance.

Where is Andrik? Keiko cried, anguished by her ignorance but determined to forfeit it only in this one particular.

Kneeling directly before you, soothed Alice B, who had perhaps guided Andrik into a paranormal hinterland as yet too ill-lit for her to follow. **But alas, you cannot cock your head to see him. Imagine Andrik beyond you, beckoning. Still, we fear, he is but a little way from where you wander importunate and grieving.**

Alice A picked up the thread of its evangelism: **I walked to and from your people's Platform, Lady Keiko, as a creature in harmony with the dictates and desires of its flesh. During this period and others like it, I was, yes, almost human, one of you in every way but the trivial and finally inconsequential one of physical appearance. Then, having learned all that time allowed and chance afforded, I ceased to come to you. It was imperative to prepare for winter transit.

At approximately the ice-heat of water, it continued after a brief pause, **a temperature that we can induce instantly within our very skulls, we think, let us say, kyberthoughts. We experience the transition to alloy-superconductivity in our secondary cerebral circuits, which *race*. Race, Lady Keiko, like photons accelerated beyond the constraining limits of the speed of light.**

As the *Heavenbridge* leaps from point to point unconstrained by Einsteinian physics?

Very well, Lady Keiko, if you like. Racing, these circuits shift our thought-phase to kybertempo, which we are designed to reach almost effortlessly, well beyond the petty pace of carnal thought.

Where was Andrik? Keiko wondered again, not having been able to see him beckoning to her in the riven twilight. Then, although she was sure that she had not projected her question at either of the aliens, Alice B responded:

We are taking him to God.

You see, fluted Alice A, in melodic glissando gloss, **still further below ice-heat, at winter-aphelion, superconductivity of our prime circuits induces yet another paracerebral phase-shift, this time to a tempo nearly coincident with that of the Control System governing all that is, and was, and will be.**

God, thought Keiko bemusedly. What did this concept of a Prime Motivator and Controller do to the Eastern belief that all beings were related to one another in harmonious hierarchies constituting a vast cosmic pattern? Given a motivator and controller above these manifold hierarchies, you could scarcely attribute either virtue or vice to the beings arrayed within each level—for in such a system behaviour arose from decrees; or from programmes, rather than from the inner dictates of each being's special nature.

The negative of an aurora wriggled like breeding black snakes through the gauze of Keiko's kybertrance sky.

How do I escape? thought Keiko, for she rejected the aliens' proof of God as harmful to the health of the fragile human soul. How do I rescue Andrik from the malaise of Kyber "spirituality"? Or are we the ones who suffer from malaise . . . ?

Speed to control tempo, or alarmingly thereabouts, our kyberthoughts permit epiphany, my sweet Lady Kei. The overreality manifests itself! We peek into the demesne of control by first having peaked into that of death-in-life and life-in-death.

Pun-*koan*! sang Alice B.

Our biobrains are cryogenically stilled by now, of course, but we thermothoughtfully warm independent portions of our flesh-brains to think these revelatory messages for you. Our secondary kybercircuits transmit said messages to your axon-aerial receivers one and a quarter million kilometres long.

Cold intelligence, operating at superspeed. Intelligence, wondered Keiko, fast in its icy captivity, *of what?*

The difference between the speed of operation of the prime circuits of our hard brain and that of the axon circuits of our soft brain, Lady Kei, is the difference between supranormal and normal perception. Our side-eyes, as you have already astutely guessed, are the instruments of vision of the hard brain. We see what outlives the flimsiness of time and fleshly bodies.

While I am blind! cried Keiko's spirit. **Andrik and I are blind, and you yourselves are doomed to melt in the dreadful blast of Dextro's nova!**

Not so. Once you yourself believed otherwise, Lady Keiko The phraseology mocked her own.

But how can you control the orbit of your world? Do you manipulate it with kyberthoughts? Or do you control the very rhythms of your suns?

There is a control system. We peek into it by peaking into what you have called death-sleep. Yes, we peek by peaking, and dream by sleeping, and scheme by speaking to ourselves with—

Please! cried Keiko in blind and mind-bound torment.

—the tongues of angels, sounding brass and silver! Forgive this alliterative, if assuredly not illiterate, recitation. There is, I repeat, a control system: the Control System. We are its experiment in knowing it, we Onogorovans. We communicate our knowledge of it, to it, in collective kybertrance—at which times we are not merely *with* it, Lady Keiko, but also *of* it. Unto the very limits of our understanding.

Andrik!

We have taken him to God, and should you likewise desire that honour, we are ready to escort your consciousness that way, too.

This invitation appalled Keiko. She threw back her head, worked to free her hands from the articulate pincers gripping them, and somehow tugged her left hand clear. The world did not immediately spring into being from the twilight chaos of kybertrance, however, and she saw that Onogoro's sky was still a negative dazzle of ivory and slate, and Andrik only a watery phantom of himself—his eyes were tiny flickering suns.

If God was a control system, God was infinitely more alien than the Kybers. You could never attain perfect union with that which lay above and beyond you, *outside* you, manipulative and dictatorial rather than serenely existent and quiescently complementary. Andrik, a Westerner, might approve the concept of such a god; but how could she—or even the cyberneticist Betti Songa, whose professional expertise encompassed the finer points of programming and control, but whose cultural background denied these same mechanistic tendencies in nature—ever surrender to so impersonal a cosmology?

We seek union, too, the Kybers told her, even though Keiko had brought her left knee up from the flagstones in an effort to disconnect her subconscious from its physical grounding in kybertrance.

Indeed, continued the alien voices, **we discontinuously *obtain* union, and much more frequently than it is given human mystics to do—because we are *designed* to approach that state.**

Then how may you take Andrik to God? She was flailing about with her left arm, desperate, sightless, cold. **He's not an Onogorovan, and neither am I!**

Alice A recaptured her hand, and Keiko was borne to earth again—to be translated with Andrik over the bridge of death-sleep to the Kybers' alien Elysium? The taste of her guide's quasi-flesh lingered on her tongue, a welcome sensation precisely to the extent that it tied her to the world beneath this bleak and dizzying bridge.

She had no human voice with which to scream.

We lead you into the presence by hymning in continent-wide chorale the paean of our Way.

I don't want—!

Switches were thrown, circuits were opened, and a sound like the intermittent burr of an overloaded transformer wracked Keiko's body through the conducting channels of her bones. She was blind, mute, deaf, desensitized to nearly every sensation but pain and fear of pain; meanwhile the Kybers were attempting—insanely, altruistically—to augment the tempo of her perception to that of a control system whose suzerainty she would never accept or acknowledge. Thousands of Kyber families poured their "voices" into the paean lifting her to God, while, bereft of Andrik and the world, she braked her burning consciousness and resisted their efforts. Her body writhed blindly between the Kybers crucifying her above the flagstones.

Let her go, crooned Alice A. **Let her go before her brittle body snaps; before, to daub us culpable, her blood spills out.**

Suddenly she was free, free of the Kyber's iron grips, free of the universal choiring that had threatened to carry her spirit into the throne room—the *control* room—of the primordial tyrant; not a deity but a system, not a unifying consciousness but a programmer.

Maybe Sixkiller had been right. Even if the Kybers were alive by all the standard biological criteria, they were self-confessedly in thrall to . . . a control system. That made them, yes, machines. Even their intelligence and free will—if you could use those loaded terms—were attributes of the system that had programmed them to know it. The next step in this inescapable chain of reasoning led you to conclude that human beings, despite not having been specifically programmed to know the primordial tyrant dictating the shapes of their lives, were likewise a variety of machine, albeit a less complex or successful variety because incapable of merging unaided with their Controller.

Or else you could assume that the God-Behind-the-Galaxies of the Kybers was not humanity's Controller at all.

This was Keiko Takahashi's instinctive assumption even as she fell back from the kneeling aliens and begged for the world to reassert itself around her. . . .

EIGHTEEN

Slowly her ordinary sight came back. There in tableau were the two kneeling Kybers, Andrik suspended between, his face and eyes aflame with the atmospheric riot of decoupling. Or, rather, the *whites* of his eyes were aflame, for his irises had rolled up into his head like a dead man's. His mouth hung open, and spittle made an icy lacework on his bottom lip. Behind him, pregnant and unmoving, the Kybers gestating new life in their joint womb, great metal icons on a bier filigreed with frost.

"Andrik!" Keiko shouted. "We've got to go back! We're leaving Onogoro, all of us!"

Alice A—Izanagi; her former pupil; once the family's septa-prime—released Andrik's hand, came gracefully out of its kneeling posture, and hoisted itself upward on its extensible limbs. It ceased growing only after attaining a height that overawed and intimidated Keiko. Its peripheral eye-bulbs diminished in size and brightness as it grew. This was no Onogorovan embodiment of Kannon but a vengeful alien saint hungry for devotion.

153

"He's there," the Kyber said gently, belying the vengefulness which Keiko had just attributed to it. "He's there."

The alien apparently meant to imply that Andrik—obviously feverish rather than supercooled, being, after all, a creature of flesh rather than of miracle metals and alloys—stood at last on the threshold of the ultimate Control Room, peering in with astonished inward eyes and longing to take the fateful metaphysical step that would unite him with the Controller even if that step extinguished the life sheltering his own microscopic spark of the divine. The Kybers had taken Andrik *there*, as far as he could go, and Keiko suddenly understood that it would be impossible to budge him from that threshold without taking back to the Platform a mere husk of the man she had loved. A zombie, one of the living dead, a straw man nodding in the ion winds of night.

Keiko's body ached. She had nearly unsocketed her left arm struggling to get free of the Kybers, and each time she took a step—as she did now, discreetly backing away from her confrontation with Alice A—a pain jolted through her side, stabbing upward beneath her ribs like a well-aimed spear or poniard. How was she ever going to get back to the floater?

"You've hurt me," she accused the alien. "I don't think you understand how badly you've hurt me."

"You're welcome, Lady Keiko," said the Kyber evenly, without a note of sarcasm, although it well understood how humans wielded that verbal weapon. "May you evolve most craftily beyond the hurts."

"Evolve . . .?"

"I am sorry only that you could not anticipate the pains that we inadvertently inflicted, in order to parry them by adjustments in advance of their disclosure. Still, we released you at your pleasure.''

"Too late," Keiko said. "Much too late."

Then, to her astonishment, the Kyber began singing—with perfect pitch and an archaic music-hall flair—one of the popular songs that she had used as an instructional aid during the early days of her involvement with the alien in the knowledge centre. *Piano Roll Blues*. An old American ditty, joyous and cornball.

" 'I want to hear it again'," crooned the Kyber, tottering toward her menacingly, "'I want to hear it again: that old piano roll blues!' "

Incongruous, incongruous.

"You are no better or worse than we, Lady Kei," said Alice A by way of explanation. "We are the notes of the piano roll of our genetipsychic heritage, after all, and so are you of yours. That which slotted the rolls and plays out our melodies on the upright piano of consensus reality is one and the same composer/ performer. Sometimes, however, we Kybers are permitted to slot the rolls and tickle the keys ourselves. You need not fear us simply because we are able to influence the performance more often than you. What we wish to do, Lady Keiko, is . . . Show You the Way."

"Kybertrance is madness," said Keiko, looking behind her. "Your death-sleep is insane. Your world view is a vile, melancholy thing. I leave you to your deaths."

"Our *Weltanschauung*, our world view, will prevent those deaths, O little teacher, or at the very least permit us to trot foxily around them."

No longer listening, Keiko shouted again at Andrik, knowing that she would not be able to rouse him. His

name—the living word—echoed in the pit, rang against
the icy rocks. Tears came to her eyes, salt in her blurred
apprehension of the night, and at last she broke and ran.

Three steps, five steps, seven.

Then Keiko, quivering and alert, halted in the first
interior spiral of the labyrinth. Looming ahead of her
were the three aliens who had earlier taken up sentry
duty around the floater. They were returning from
work, tall mahogany-and-metal sylphs glowing blue
about their halo-crests, radiant with the Onogorovan
equivalent of St Elmo's fire. They came toward her in
stately procession, amiable, inexorable, strange.
Her heart began to pound, and she retreated to the
atrium of the Kyber palace wondering what had happened to Sixkiller and Captain Hsi.

Fearful of what the aliens might do to her now that
she had rejected kybertrance as an agency of either
revelation or human growth, she sidled along the atrium's wall hoping to conceal herself just long enough
to let the Kybers enter; then she would dart past them
into the maze. Alice A, her student and would-be mentor, regarded her indulgently, the set of its lips conveying an aloof, alien humour. With one outstretched arm
draped with ragged kyberflesh, it resembled a Meiji Era
geisha in a tumbledown tea house.

"Goodbye, Lady Keiko," it said. "I am very
pleased to have met you." It then shut itself off; "died"
as Andrik might have said; descended into death-sleep
to meet its maker . . .

Keiko looked up. Drifting toward the atrium under
the pyrotechnic barrage of the sky was the floater. It
played blinding searchlights across the entire landscape, then maneuvred into position above the
Kyber palace as if Sixkiller was testing the finesse and
delicacy of his touch at the controls. Keiko stared. The

spindly legs of the aircraft swayed from side to side about fifteen metres overhead, glinting like giant lag screws in the auroral glare. Arctic gusts buffeted the floater occasionally, but none with enough force to dislodge it from its hover.

The the hatch came open, and she saw Captain Hsi braced inside the opening paying out the rope ladder of bonded silicon whiskers.

The ladder unravelled soundlessly in a swift, switchbacking fall—like a double strand of linked glass beads "clattering" against each other in absolute vacuum. The bottom rung of the ladder swung back and forth several steps from Keiko, about a forearm's length above her head. She hurried to clutch it, to pull herself out of the atrium with her good right arm. Her other arm, she knew, was going to be no help whatever.

"Dr Norn!" shouted Captain Hsi from the floater's hatch. "Get Dr Norn, too! We can't leave Onogoro without him!"

"There's no helping it, sir! We'll have to!"

She leapt and caught the ladder's bottom rung. The ladder itself, having fallen into the shape for which it was designed, was rigid now, supportive of her weight—but, alarmingly, she did not have enough strength in her right arm to pull herself any higher.

Helpless, she dangled.

The Kybers were coming, the remainder of Alice A's family. Turning her head, Keiko saw that the three mechanized sylphs who had guarded the floater on the ridge were pushing into the atrium together. Even though they resembled geese hurrying to get through the same gate, a formidable panic seized her. They were coming to capture her as Andrik had been captured, and if she could not escape them now, no hope of future escape would ever sustain her—for she would exist beyond the pale of hope. Gritting her teeth, she chinned herself even with the ladder's bottom rung, only to find that her entire strength had lapsed.

"Hang on!" shouted Captain Hsi. "I'll pull you up!" Braced in the opening, he attempted to haul the ladder in like a fisherman hauling a net, his own heavy coat an encumbrance too bulky to overcome.

"Tell Sixkiller to lift us out of here!" Keiko cried.

Captain Hsi shouted, "If he lifts us up and you fall, you'll be killed!"

She felt alien pincers under her arms, a pair of armoured hands whose grip was irresistible. Keiko screamed, and the floater's hanging ladder buckled and twisted as she was dragged away from it.

Her right hand released the rung, and the ladder snapped back into place, sparkling glassily.

Captain Hsi stood up in the hatch opening, his face contorted, a cry frozen in his throat. Whatever he was shouting or trying to shout was lost upon Keiko, who relaxed like a rabbit in the devouring jaws of the wolf, regretfully acquiescent.

"Goodbye, Lady Keiko," crooned the Kyber who held her, lifting her to the ladder and placing her on its penultimate rung. "I am very pleased to have met you."

She scrambled up the ladder in the stinging cold, her mind empty of either fear or wonder. Then she paused to look down briefly on Andrik. He was dead to her, frost-bitten, a tiny figure kneeling in prayer with a Kyber. Gutted now of his human personality, perhaps he was at one with a god that she could not believe in. Was there tragedy in that? Maybe the tragedy was ultimately her own, for not being able to believe . . .

"Climb!" shouted Captain Hsi. "Come on, *climb*!"

Keiko obeyed—as did Sixkiller, who had apparently

assumed that the captain's command was meant for him.

The floater rose into the night. Glancing down as it ascended, Keiko surveyed the upturned faces of the aliens: Alice A in eloquent catatonia, Andrik dwindling to a shadow beside the death-sleeping Alice B, and the spirals of the labyrinth opening ever outward like an immense stone rose. She closed her eyes.

Virtually one-handed, she hastened up the silicon ladder. Only when Captain Hsi grasped the utility epaulets on her parka and dragged her into the floater did she open her eyes again.

Then the ladder was reeled in, and the hatch slammed shut.

Inside the floater perched head over knees in her seat, Keiko found that beneath her heavy clothes she was running with sweat. Her teeth chattered, and her temples knocked with a noise like water sloshing against a pier.

"Welcome back," said Sixkiller laconically. "What happened?"

"Andrik's gone," she responded, not wanting to talk. Still, she forced herself to ask, "What happened to you?"

"I don't know exactly. Our Kyber sentries abandoned their posts and went traipsing together back into their maze. So we got airborne lickety-split and came looking for you. We were afraid——" He stopped.

Captain Hsi, after a moment, said, "I am holding you personally accountable for the loss of Dr Norn, Dr Takahashi. Had you performed your duties as duty itself dictated, he would never have succeeded in coming out here. Had you comported yourself in accordance with both regulations and common sense, it's highly unlikely that——"

"Sir," put in Sixkiller abruptly.

The captain blinked. "It's highly unlikely," he resumed, "that Dr Norn would have—"

"Sir!"

"What is it, Mr Sixkiller?" the captain snapped, irritated.

"Shut up," Sixkiller told him. "Let's all just keep our mouths shut until we get back to the Platform."

Keiko did not look up. She rubbed her temples with her fingers and stared at the featureless white floorboarding.

Meanwhile, their floater skimmed over the surface of the world that had inexplicably given rise to the Kybers. Laevo appeared in the heavens like a lighthouse beacon in a season of hurricane, deathly white in spite of its promise of deliverance.

NINETEEN

When they set down on the Platform Craig Olivant and
Betti Songa were waiting just beyond the landing area,
anxious to learn how they had fared and to impart some
startling news of their own.

Keiko was the first to exit the floater. She embraced
Betti on the wind-swept decking and extended a gloved
hand to Craig. The captain and Sixkiller clambered out
into the night more reservedly, like caged creatures
sceptical of the advantages of release.

"Dismantle the floater," Captain Hsi commanded
Sixkiller. "Get a Platform mech, take the floater apart,
and pack it aboard the shuttle."

"All right," the pilot said. He glanced at Keiko's
professional colleagues with undisguised curiosity,
then headed for the observatory to find a mechanic to
help disassemble the aircraft.

They had been gone from the Platform not quite two
hours. In three more, their entire expeditionary party
was supposed to bid Onogoro farewell for ever.

"Andrik?" Betti Songa asked.

161

Keiko found that she was weeping openly, shaking her head and clutching Craig's monstrous hand as if it were her lifeline to everything warm, familiar, human. She had never felt especially close to the astrophysicist before, however, and she was conscious of a tinge of bewilderment in his readiness to support and solace. Betti, too, kept an arm around Keiko. The bearlike blond American and the pert black Tanzanian, her comfort on a strange planet; human beings; friends. For a long time no one spoke, and Keiko's tears crystallized in her lashes and on the high planes of her cheeks. Like a warder awaiting the moment when he can return his prisoner to her cell, Captain Hsi hung back.

Craig released Keiko's hand. "Captain Hsi," he said, "there's a group of Kybers at the base of the Platform, near the elevator riser."

"Kybers?" the captain exclaimed. "What are they doing here?"

"I think they want to come up. We locked the elevator capsule in place not long—well, not long after Andrik must have left us. The door at the foot of the riser's tight, too—they can't get up here unless we countermand the locks and extend an invitation."

"But what do they want?"

"I think they realize we're leaving, sir. I'm sure they do. The ones who have presented themselves here want us to take them off-planet. They're seeking asylum aboard the *Heavenbridge*. Don't ask me whether it's political, religious, or biological asylum, though—they just want our help."

"Defectors? Alien defectors?"

"Yes, sir. That's how it looks."

"We have to take them," Betti Songa said, facing the captain without removing her arm from Keiko's waist. "We have to take as many as we can, at least.

There may be more coming," gesturing sweepingly, "from out there, from too far away to get here before we're ready to go."

"More?" Inside the plush ring of his hood, Captain Hsi raised his thin eyebrows; his eyes bulged noticeably in the electric glow of the colliding solar winds. Then he lowered his head and, signalling the others to follow, made for the Platform's forward railing.

Keiko, at Betti's silent urging, tagged after the men. At the rail she was astonished to see several incomplete Kyber families picking their way through the boulders and the great purplish pseudo-boulders toward the Platform. She counted fourteen individuals in three separate groups, each group negotiating a different isthmus of frost-inscribed rock. The Kybers' bright ligneous haloes moved from side to side like tracking discs, and their legs collapsed or extended so that their heads appeared to float along at a single unvarying altitude despite the unevenness of the terrain. Under the prismatic arc of the auroras the aliens' promenade struck Keiko as dreamlike and vaguely threatening.

"Of course," said Craig, "you can't see the ones already under the Platform. The monitors in the observatory suggest we've got about five down there, patiently waiting for official approval of their petition. Naomi's been talking with them through the intercom system, or with one of them, anyway. All that's really clear is that they want to escape the consequences of Dextro's going nova. They know—every single Onogorovan does—that we're leaving tonight, and these are the ones who want to entrust their lives and future security to us."

"O Kybers of little faith," intoned Keiko plaintively.

"Defectors," said Captain Hsi again.

"Yes, sir," Betti Songa interjected. "But it's surprising only because we had implicitly begun to assume that the Kybers are less a species of autonomous individuals than a kind of vast computer intelligence whose units are simply parts of a governing whole. That's what *I* had begun to assume, anyway. What Keiko and Andrik told us about their first conversations with the aliens certainly suggested that the personalities of the Kybers were interchangeable. Which is why it's hard to accept the idea that these creatures do have distinct personalities, and that it's possible for them to come to decisions different from those dictated by a majority of their kind . . . Yes, sir, that's a fitting way to put it—these Kybers are defectors."

Keiko considered, her hands gripping the Platform's rail and her mind casting out to the alien palace where Andrik had willingly forfeited his humanity. If the Kybers were the experiments of a faceless and spiritless control system operating at superspeed to keep at least this part of the cosmos functioning smoothly—through pain's periodic crisis, and the promise of imminent destruction—then even these "defectors" owed that system their allegiance. They did its bidding in spite of themselves. They were programmed for obedience, and all their intelligence, ingenuity, and savvy ultimately rebounded to that end. How much free will does an automaton have?

By simple definition, none.

"We have to take as many as we can," Betti Songa was saying.

"No!" Keiko blurted. Then she flushed, aware that by a route rather different from that taken by Sixkiller she had nevertheless arrived at a xenophobia as virulent as the pilot's.

"What's the matter?" Craig asked her.

"I don't believe they're defecting. I believe they're here at the behest of the others, who see us as yet another survival option—although not so good an option as the exercise of prayerful control in kyber-trance."

"What's wrong with that?" Craig wondered aloud. "We *are* a survival option."

"The problem is that it's not defection, it's . . ." She hesitated.

"What? What is it, Kei?"

"It's infiltration," she told the astrophysicist. "They'll go back with us, if we let them, in order to colonize Earth for a new variety of kyberlife. That's what their survival option amounts to finally: they hope to displace us, replace us, take over—because they have evolved beyond us here on Onogoro, under heaven's bridge, and they see no hope of our ever putting a foot on that span if left to ourselves."

"They're technologically backwards!" Craig exclaimed. "You're fabricating motives they couldn't possibly have."

Said Betti Songa gently, "You sound like Sixkiller, Kei."

"They're their own technology," Keiko responded, still feverish, uncertain of her ground but determined to test it. "They don't need starships, refrigerators, oscil-loscopes, motorcars, any of that diverse and complex gadgetry! They're their own technology, which means they're so sophisticated, so advanced, that we wrongly perceive their culture as primitive!" She caught her breath and looked at Betti and Craig in turn. "Besides, you weren't out there. *Neither of you was out there*."

"Viewed objectively, their culture *is* primitive," Craig countered. "Human beings aren't replaceable by Kybers. Surely even they understand that. The motives you impute to them just don't wash, Kei.''

"Their culture is internalized, shared broadly across the entire spectrum of Kyber society, and these petitioners that Captain Hsi calls defectors are here at the bidding of the general will!''

"Which is fine,'' said Betti. "Which is altogether fine, Kei.''

At that moment, Sixkiller exited the central balloon of the observatory with a Platform mech. Captain Hsi brusquely hailed the floater pilot, calling him over to their group.

"How many Kybers could we take aboard the shuttle to the *Heavenbridge* without sacrificing necessary equipment or personnel?''

"Am I necessary personnel?'' Sixkiller asked. "Is Dr Takahashi?''

"You know what I mean, Mr Sixkiller. How many Kybers could we realistically carry aloft from the Platform?''

"I don't know.''

"Roughly, Mr Sixkiller! Roughly!''

"Considering that we're pretty heavily packed for this last run, no more than a single family—roughly. Less than seven if we're being really 'realistic'. None if we're being safe. Are we *actually* going to take home representatives of the local sentient life form as souvenirs? Jesus!''

"We'll take home the ones who are already at the central riser,'' said Captain Hsi. "There's nothing we can do for the others.''

Keiko's heart shifted in her breast. "Sir—'' she began, chagrined to find herself supporting Sixkiller's cynical position out of a fear as demeaning and cowardly as his. "Sir, there's a Control that dictates what they do. If they come home with us, it will eventually dictate what we do, too.''

"God," said Craig Olivant, and Keiko was unable to tell whether he was defining that Control or simply despising her fear.

What Betti Songa whispered to her then, apparently in an attempt to soothe and console her, was even more chilling than the possibility of Craig's contempt: "Perhaps, Keiko, we will then begin to fulfil our destiny as a species. Hush now. Hush. We must do what the moment demands.''

"Only five or six," said Captain Hsi. "If they give birth only every thousand years or so, it will be very difficult for the Kybers to replace humanity as the dominant sapient species on Earth.'' He smiled dismissively at Keiko.

TWENTY

But she was not so easily dismissed.

"Wait. You forgot something."

"Indeed? I should have thought, on the contrary, that it is you who have forgotten not only your duty but the etiquette appropriate to your present status!"

Keiko went on doggedly: "There are five Kybers down below. Entrust their lives? Their security? Five, Captain Hsi! They've just abandoned their own unborn child! They've left behind the pair who are locked in paracybergamic union. They've run out on the birth. What kind of trust and security is that? What sort of survival? I don't believe it. Whatever has sent them marching here with this phoney request is something that supersedes questions of ordinary individual survival. It has to be something collective that—"

Captain Hsi cut her off. "As you said. Perhaps it is simply the height—or should I say nadir?—of individualism to run out on your offspring. Indeed, this reassures me still more. How can there ever be more than five of them, however long they live! They have

169

conveniently neutered themselves.'' Hsi paced about the ice-furred decking. ''Still, while I complain about dereliction of duty in one direction, should I condone an even more shameful performance by our world-be guests?''

''Exactly,'' said Sixkiller, locking eyes with Keiko as though to mesmerize her.

Betti spoke up: ''I hardly think we can prescribe standards of ethical behaviour for aliens.''

Naomi Davis, who had stepped out of the observatory in time to catch the last few exchanges, said bluntly, ''Fried baby is no baby.''

Sixkiller swung about. ''Oh, and I suppose that five adult Kybers couldn't have managed to pick up the other two and brought them along? It would hardly seem much of an athletic feat, would it?''

Naomi opened her mouth to reply.

''Don't look at me,'' said Sixkiller hastily. ''You might like a well-balanced Kyber ecology on board, but I'm not going to be your ambulance man to ensure it.''

''Maybe they assumed that lift-off would be too much of a strain,'' suggested Craig Olivant. ''For the foetus, I mean.''

''Oh, you contradict yourself beautifully!'' cried Keiko. ''First they have a primitive culture, but now they know all about G-forces!''

''Surely you pumped enough technical manuals into your student for them to work that one out, Kei. Would you take your pregnant wife riding up to orbit?'' Craig faltered, embarrassed. ''I mean, if you—''

''Anyway,'' put in Betti Songa diplomatically, ''they may have rigid customs associated with the birthing. We still have our share of them. Maybe the pregnant parents are not permitted to travel under any circumstances—they have to stay in the hut.''

But Keiko was thinking not of abandoned pregnant wives but of an abandoned ''husband'', pregnant with knowledge, undergoing a variety of labour pain which she—for a while—had shared. Stillborn Andrik, dead while trying to give birth to himself . . .

Sixkiller smiled in a way that struck Keiko as wicked, as if determined to complicate the argument further—so that the ensuing delay would thwart the Kybers' effort to come aboard. ''How do we know,'' he asked, ''that those five down below *are* all from one family, minus the pregnant parents? How do we know they aren't from separate families, and aren't all pregnant themselves? Suppose they wrenched themselves away from the other supportive parent, who may—for all we know—simply function as a sort of extrasomatic energy-source or placenta. How do we know we aren't proposing carrying Kyber within Kyber back to Earth?''

''That's nonsense,'' snapped Naomi. ''I've seen your holos of that couple on their bier. They're—''

''Inseparable,'' said Sixkiller, turning aside. ''How touching.''

Captain Hsi waved a hand. ''Enough of this. I shall interview these Kyber suppliants before we grant them passage. They shall, for once, explain themselves fully. See to it, Mr Sixkiller, then carry on with that floater.''

Soon the five Kybers had ascended the Platform's central riser to the deck, and the elevator capsule was locked into place again. A second incomplete family had already arrived below by now, and indeed had been there for some minutes. Meanwhile, the other two renegade groups that Keiko had counted from the rail were just now—she saw—disappearing beneath the Platform.

None too soon, she thought anxiously. Although, in another sense, far too late.

As the Kybers followed the pilot toward Captain Hsi, Keiko told herself that there was something odd about one of the refugees. One of its arms looked—yes, out of joint. And it moved less smoothly than the other aliens, virtually limping in their wake.

"Sir," called one of the Platform mechs, emerging from the observatory.

"Not now," barked Captain Hsi. "We're falling behind schedule. Lend Mr Sixkiller a hand."

The mech trotted obediently to the pilot's side, then followed him to the floater where another mech was already at work. Sixkiller's new assistant said something to him which made the pilot start and frown. It looked as if he might come back in their direction—but he changed his mind and set about dismantling the craft, albeit with a portion of his attention apparently upon the Captain's interview, straining against the wind to hear what was being said.

Captain Hsi squared up to the Kyber quintet, who had halted before him as a single individual.

"Are you all from one family?"

"We have no family now but you, if you will have us," replied the Kyber who was marginally to the fore. The spokes of its halo glittered in the wash of the arc-lights by which Sixkiller and the mechs were working.

"But you left two of you behind, isn't that so?"

"Indeed. How could we be of *your* family, had we not?"

"What about them? What happens to them?"

"Away alone alost aloved alorn," piped a second Kyber voice. "They lie dead on the bier, later to awake."

"We have left their wake," crooned the alien whose arm looked to be unsocketed.

Captain Hsi glanced irritably at Keiko, but could not bring himself, she supposed, to ask for a gloss.

"We ask refuge," said the leader. "We beg sanctuary. Grant us asylum. Please take us with you, out of all this."

"Asylum?" asked the captain, seizing on the word. "Of what sort?"

"From the burning of the sun, from the burden of our people."

"What burden? Surely it must lie on all of you if it has to do with the coming nova. How can you make an individual choice—you five—when your entire species shares a common mind? Or has this choice been made *for* you? Are you really free to act apart from the others?"

"A joint mind need not be common, O Captain."

Captain Hsi shuddered in his coat and shook his head. "We don't have time for this, my fine Kyber. Out there in your palaces you may play word games, but here," gesturing at the access gantry beside the shuttle, "here is the moment of truth. You will pay for your passage, or you will remain on Onogoro."

Keiko saw that over by the gantry Sixkiller, having put the mechs to work, was weighing the risks of approaching the captain again. At last he made up his mind and fought the wind toward them.

"Excuse me, sir, but there's something you should probably know."

"And what is that?" said Captain Hsi, turning slightly aside from the aliens.

"One of the mechs," nodding back toward them, "was in the observatory just before this group came up. While they were still waiting, and after another group of five had showed up, he followed the interaction of the two groups on the monitor screen. He says—" Sixkiller stuck, as if to heighten the captain's suspense.

"Yes?"

"He says that the new arrivals were squabbling with this tribe."

"About who should get aboard the refugee ship?"

"It looked more as if they were trying to pull them away, back into Kyberland. But they weren't trying too hard. It looked—to the mech's way of thinking—like a performance. An act."

Betti Songa addressed Captain Hsi: "He's attempting to suggest that the Kybers are aggressive, sir—that we have something else to fear from them. The truth, though, is that we have no evidence that any Kyber has ever assaulted another."

"They restrained me," said Keiko unenthusiastically. She tried to find the Kyber with the unsocketed arm, which it had probably injured in whatever awkward melee had occurred below. If any had. Perhaps the mech reporting that disturbance had misinterpreted what he saw. However, the Kyber in question seemed to have completely repaired itself, maybe by some internal retensioning of wires and micropulleys.

"They restrained the floater," added Sixkiller. "They interfered."

"That isn't aggression," protested Betti.

Captain Hsi turned back to the waiting Kybers. "Why did you quarrel down there?"

"We are now a broken family. When one of us dies forever, also this breaking occurs. Be assured that this is the only kind of violence we know. When a second broken family arrived below, the urge to be whole again—to become sevenfold—overcame a few of their diminished number. There was among them a yearning to form a septa, which urge our own broken family must resist—for it might have drawn us back from sanctuary.''

"Some element of the collective will was involved," hazarded the captain. "Does the collective will wish you to stay or to leave?"

"Sir, it was a put-on," insisted Sixkiller. "A performance."

Keiko wanted to shout at the obstinate man, but at that moment a cry from the mech up on the access gantry interrupted them: "Sir, more of them are turning up! Fifteen or so! And the others—the ones under the Platform—they're coming out! Hell, they're climbing one another's shoulders, trying to reach the deck!"

Captain Hsi ran with the others to the railing. Keiko drew up behind him, panting in the cold.

The other Kybers who had come for sanctuary, or for some arcane purpose of their own, had indeed formed a spindly siege tower out of their own bodies. As Keiko and her fellow expedition members watched, the boom-like arms of one alien reached down to hoist yet another Kyber aloft, positioning and then propping it atop their living column, where it ultimately stood upright. This last Kyber's crested head was only five or six metres below the Platform's deck level, but it was looking down at its fellows rather than up at the astonished humans. The structure which it capped was perfectly balanced, even as the Kybers' bodies methodically elongated toward their goal.

Another alien languidly ascended the stack.

Sixkiller unholstered his laser and leaned out.

"All right," whispered Captain Hsi. "Go ahead."

As this final Kyber perched on the shoulders of the alien now beneath him and pistoned its weird body upward, simultaneously extending his arms toward the Platform rail, the pilot fired. "Thus falls Babel!" he cried, squeezing the thinnest line of coherent light down at the base of the alien pyramid. Not, as Keiko had suspected he would do, at the Kyber reaching toward them with its imploring arms.

Indeed, the pilot tracked the laser beam carefully across a jumble of frosted rocks until it intersected a leg. The leg flared and fell away. Slowly, then the spindly pylon of bodies also began to fall—outwards, away from the Expeditionary Platform.

As if in a dream, however, the topmost Kyber boosted itself upward from its fellows—a powerful, thrusting leap. Its hands closed like padlocks around the uprights of the railing, and it chinned itself up until it was level with their feet.

Sixkiller directed his laser at its face.

"No!" shouted Naomi. "Don't murder it!"

"The goddamn thing is asking for more than murder!" Sixkiller replied, turning a look of baleful hatred on Keiko's friend.

Naomi grasped his wrist.

He broke the woman's grip and pointed the laser directly at the Kyber's head. His body shook with ill-suppressed rage.

"Please do not kill me," said the alien with irrational placidity. "Grant me the sanctuary you have given to the others."

The pylon of Kybers that had toppled dreamily to the ground was now disentangling itself into separate beings, apparently undamaged. Keiko watched them sort themselves out. The one whose leg the pilot had severed stood up on its remaining leg like a flamingo; it stayed in this position, reproachfully, while all the others—dissuaded from any further assault on the Platform—began to filter slowly away into the icy mists, oddly acquiescent in their failure. What of the last one? Keiko wondered. Would it attempt to hop after them, an impossible pogo-stick being?

After a moment or two Captain Hsi asked, "Did those others," nodding after them, "want sanctuary, too?" Perhaps he was hoping that the Kyber's grip would slacken and it would fall, thus disposing of the problem of dealing with it. The Kyber disappointed him, however.

"They quit too easily," said Sixkiller. "Genuine living creatures with their hearts in it, would have rioted."

"Maybe they were only attempting to bring the defectors home," said Betti. "I mean, the majority of them were—but it wasn't worth losing any personnel."

"Well?" Captain Hsi demanded of the clinging Kyber.

"Yes, very," responded the alien. "Thank you. May I join you and the others of my kind, whom you so kindly save?"

"I asked if those others also wanted sanctuary."

"I want it. The others have accepted their destiny, and it is too late to call them back and inquire of them their private preferences. There is a time for leaving and a time for cleaving, and never the twain shall meet."

Stymied by this verbal foolishness, the captain looked away. "Our time for leaving is now," he said, perceiving that the Platform mechs had nearly finished dismantling and stowing the floater. "We're late." Abruptly, his questions still unanswered, he made up his mind. "Climb over. You may come with us. Mr Sixkiller, see the six of them on board the shuttle."

As the Kyber scaled the railing and strode to join the others, Naomi Davis hugged Keiko to her protectively, maternally. "We're going home," she whispered. "Isn't it good to be going home?"

"Andrik," Keiko murmured.

"There's no way to fetch him back, child. No way, no time. He's where he chose to go. Remember that. He's where he chose to go."

Keiko wondered where exactly that was, and if her absent lover had survived the journey.

Her last view of Onogoro, on the screen in the crowded passenger cabin, showed the solitary Kyber whose right leg Sixkiller's laser had amputated still standing in the same position on the rimed rock beneath the dwindling, abandoned Platform. Apparently it couldn't hop away like a pogo stick—though surely it could have dragged itself the few metres to where its severed leg lay, to use this as a crutch, a peg-legged pirate marooned on an island threatened by volcanism. The alien stood unmoving, perfectly balanced. No way forward, no way back. Perhaps it had died, switched itself off . . .

As the shuttle rose, and the Platform and the Kyber diminished, it did not raise its arm in farewell. Was there no real farewell to Onogoro? She searched briefly for the ruined palace where Andrik's mortal body was, but she could not find it; and then they were too high.

TWENTY-ONE

Aboard the *Heavenbridge* the Kybers travelled in a chamber aft of the central passenger nacelle. Immediately after their arrival in orbit, Sixkiller had escorted them—an even half dozen—to this auxiliary cargo hold, and persuaded them that the trip to Earth would be more comfortably spent in kybertrance than in a state of useless wakefulness. After all, Captain Hsi, for logistic as well as security reasons, was not going to permit them to explore the ship and they would be confined to the cargo room for the duration of the voyage. Fortunately, the trip would take only about five standard months, and they were cybergamically equipped with a cold-sleep ability not available to their human counterparts.

Thus had Sixkiller mercifully murdered his charges.

Keiko passed the first half of the return journey sleeping or sitting cross-legged on the low bunk in her cabin. Overtures from Naomi, Betti, and even Farrell Sixkiller to leave her insular haven occasionally, in order to join the others in either research assessment or recreational small talk, she politely turned aside. Her cabin became her cosmos and no one sought to pick the quintessential Keiko Takahashi out of the shell she had made of it. She would not be swayed, and, besides, she appeared often enough at meals and other obligatory gatherings to disabuse both the ship's medics and her closest frineds of the suspicion that she was lapsing into autism. Keiko's problem, they resolutely assured one another, was grief, old-fashioned grief; time was the only effective cure—for which reasons they more or less permitted her to indulge the fierce but perplexing whims of her bereavement.

As the *Heavenbridge* drew closer to its programmed emergence point beyond the orbit of Pluto, dreams terrifyingly reminiscent of the muffled sensory effects of kybertrance began to plague Keiko. A portion of her consciousness would convince her sleeping self that she was back on Onogoro, in the trapezoidal atrium of a Kyber palace, her hands linked with those of two imposing aliens, Andrik directly opposite her with pinwheeling suns for eyes and an envelope of luminous plasma for a body. The sky shone like the monochrome thermograph of a cancer, and the maze in which she knelt was a labyrinth of spiralling darkness. Andrik's voice never got through to her in these dreams, but occasionally—more and more often the closer the *Heavenbridge* came to the Sol system—Keiko believed that she heard the irreducible uptempo whine of the Intelligence-Behind-Creation. It sought to synch with, and thereby overmaster, the rhythms of her own terrified consciousness; and she feared that if It were successful in this attempt, she would achieve not union with Absolute Godhead but extinction in the compulsive drone of its stereotypical mantra: OMMMMMMMMMMMMMMM.

One sleep-period, then, Keiko awoke from an involuntary sojourn in the territories of kybertrance to find that resonances from this realm continued to haunt her: echoes, afterimages, displaced fragrances. They seemed to emanate from somewhere aboard the *Heavenbridge* rather than from her own disrupted dreams, and she left the cabin to seek out their source, knowing only too well that she would have to go to the cargo hold where the Kybers stood against one bulkhead in inadvertent parody of the statues of Kannon at Sanjusangendo.

No one passed her in the corridor, and she entered the auxiliary cargo chamber aft of the main body of the ship with trembling hands and a pervasive dread insufficient to deter her from her purpose. The Kybers—not quite a family—did not move as she slid the door to behind her. The fact that they were closer to human-scale than she had ever seen them (a condition dictated by the hold's low ceiling) bled away a little of her fear and made them seem approachable if not wholly familiar.

Between the sleek curtain of a collapsed inflatable and several crates of Onogorovan rocks, Keiko threaded a path to the bulkhead against which the Kybers were noncommittally arrayed. They were "dead", without doubt. Was it possible that one of them, or all of them together, had infected the stuff of her dreams with their own spirit-nullifying concept of God the Controller . . .?

"I'm here," Keiko announced quietly. "I'm here."

Yes, it was like talking to statues. Truth to tell, the images of Kannon in the Hall of Mercy had seemed more responsive than these inscrutable zombie beings. Whereas the bodhisattvas had serenely accepted a pilgrim's heartfelt reverence, the Kybers merely occupied space and dreamt their own mini-deaths. Was that a fair comparison? Keiko had no idea. She noticed that the lateral eye-bulbs of every one of the aliens were eerily dilated, bright with some shared inner conviction.

"What have you been trying to do to me?" she demanded. "You've taken Andrik. What do you want with me?"

A click, like a key turning in a lock.

Keiko started at the sound, which had come not from the cargo hold's sliding door but from the aliens standing three abreast and two deep directly in front of her. The head of the central Kyber on the front row swivelled to one side, like that of an amusement-park mannequin or animatron, in order to fix her in its vision. Then its head purred almost soundlessly back to its original position, and its front-facing pupils began to enlarge.

"Here," it said. It extended its mailed fists toward her, then opened its hands in a gesture obviously meant to invite her to clasp them.

"I tried to go down that road with your people once before," Keiko told the alien. "I didn't get very far, though. My escorts were, well, clumsy."

"You lacked the proper frame of mind, Lady Keiko."

"A Western frame of mind? Andrik betrayed me—betrayed *us*—because of an engrained cultural bias to which many of the others on this mission are probably susceptible, too."

"Whereas your own cultural bias permits you to resist Ultimate Reality?"

"It *isn't* real, this dream you live!"

"The Real is, Lady Keiko. Ultimate Reality is. Accept my hands, and I will show you how we Kybers evolve ourselves in response to the promise of pain bestowed upon us by the God-Behind-the-Galaxies."

Torn, Keiko hesitated.

"Please," urged the Kyber, its voice (she realized) a breathy duplicate of her own. The long slender fingers flexed invitingly.

She accepted the invitation.

The auxiliary hold and all its jumbled contents disappeared. As in the Kyber palace, she was blind, trapped in a dimensionless film of oil that glittered about its edges but glared blackly at its heart. She was the contracting pupil of a Cyclops's eye, and there was a fire in that outer darkness that sought to burn her to a last combustible cinder. This happened, and the universe immediately began to reshape itself from the residues of her inner vision. She ceased to struggle against the metamorphosis, knowing that like everything else it was only temporary . . .

The hands of the Kyber were cold, cold.

Dextro burns when Laevo interposes itself between planet and blast, the alien hymned in death-sleep, ** but the carriers of each Kyber family—from whom we here aboard the *Heavenbridge* have divorced ourselves—lie conjoined in the biocybernetic pursuit of survival.**

While you survive by fleeing,Keiko thought.

She envisioned a negative of herself moving dreamily through the corridors of the light-skimmer . . . to a room that is a replica of the Kyber palace in which she helplessly abandoned Andrik. Sliding the door shut behind her, she finds that she is in just such a palace on Onogoro itself, but a shadow-Onogoro whose solidity is a function of her own altered consciousness and whose colours are white, silver, and black. There are no other colours. She is escorted by the Kyber whose hands she held in another continuum . . .

While we survive by fleeing, it echoed her. **However, attend the birth of one of our saviour offspring, whom we have directed *in vivo* toward the evolutionary end of our on-planet survival, every Kyber mind shaping its family's foetus at the impetus of an impending evil but in accordance with the will of God. Yes: Lady Keiko, attend one of our births. *Laborare est orare*. Our labour is our prayer.**

So, in either hybertrance or a vivid approximation of that alien state, Keiko attended.

Her escort leads her to the foot of the bier on which the pregnant Kybers lie back to back, their bodies fused. Here she watches—for hours, days, years—as the creatures heave rhythmically toward the birthing of a "saviour offspring". Finally the babe emerges, parting the fused lips of its parents' external genitalia and sliding in acute slow-motion into the hands of the Kyber who has led her to this place.

The scene is grainy in Keiko's vision, prohibitively distanced somehow; and yet she sees that the babe is more metal than flesh, with an immense silver casque of a head. Its lateral pupils throw out wall-eyed beams of light as thick as any human wrist, as though its first act in the world is not to drink in perceived data with newly opened eyes but rather to *shed* data— instructions, information, perceptions from a realm beyond incarnate reality—to shed these like a metaphysical beacon, thus steering the passage of ships in the stormy night that is the world.

This Kyber is the newest model. Its body armour sheaths its tiny limbs. When Keiko's midwife-guide lifts the infant toward the midnight occlusion of Dextro (a sun behind a sun, nova in labour), the limbs slide out like star points and the babe burns above its alien deliverer in retake of that fabled night in Bethlehem. All over the planet this is happening, a thousand incandescent robot Baby Jesuses signalling their own advent . . .

What did this mean? Was flesh-life not merely a way-station but an error? Had the Programmer decided—comparing Kyber with human feedback—that the most excellent, perfect denizens of its cosmos must be another sort of life entirely?

At last the irreality of kybertrance began to break up for Keiko, killed by the miracle to which she had just been an out-of-time witness; meanwhile the cargo hold reasserted its existence. The Kyber released her hands. She opened her eyes, and the dream of the previous moment flickered in her consciousness like a memory from childhood.

"I don't believe that," Keiko said. "I don't believe what you've just given me to see."

"We wanted you to know that we will survive on Onogoro," the alien told her aloud. "Even on a world cut adrift from a fevered sun."

"And Andrik?"

"Andrik thinks us—prays us—toward that survival, too, by obeying the cosmic process whose purpose is continuous acquisition of knowledge at the goad of either pain or its promise."

"To what end? For what reward?" Keiko cried, again aware of the dingy clutter around her—for the alien seemed to be retreating from her, withdrawing inexorably into the bleak winter light of kybertrance.

"Awareness," crooned the Kyber. "Perception of the Presence. These are their own rewards."

"But will Andrik survive? Will he live through what's happened and what's going to happen?"

"He?"

"His spirit," Keiko emended. "His essence."

"In our offspring saviours, yes. Assuredly. Have no fear."

"Then why do you come to Earth? Why?"

The Kyber's arms folded in toward its body and crossed each other at chest height. Its front-facing pupils dimmed and diminished, never having been particularly bright to begin with, while its lateral eye-bulbs shone like those of the infant prophesied in Keiko's recent approximation of death-sleep.

A cargo hold of the *Heavenbridge* had become, willy-nilly, a makeshift temple for the ungodly harbingers of a child—thousands of children, really—imagined into provisional existence by the Control System to which they were slave. How could Keiko, or any other human being, worship such chilling embodiments of the Kybers' enslavement? Given these bleak conditions, a deity was only a cunning chain of data, and a living mortal, whether human or alien, only a finite process, whirring toward oblivion . . .

"Ah, you've come to inspect the skeletons in our communal closet."

Keiko turned around, not really surprised that Farrell Sixkiller had managed to insinuate himself into the cargo hold without her hearing. He was light of foot, stealthiness as natural to him as breathing.

"How long have you been there?"

"I just came in." He raised an eyebrow, canted his chin. "Why? You're not embarrassed to be found in their company, are you?"

"It's more congenial than some."

"Even when they're dead? Not a peep out of them since we left the Gemini system. These days, Dr Takahashi, it's even possible to put a stethoscope to their pocket-watch tickers without risking a behead-

ing.'' He came through the narrow aisle between the
crates and the great yellow curtain of the collapsed
inflatable. "Look." He tapped his forefinger against
the halocrest of the alien to whom Keiko had just been
talking. "See there. No reflex, no response. The only
good Kyber is one whose plug has been pulled. These
are *excellent* Kybers, Dr Takahashi.''

"So what do you think has happened to them, Farrell?''

"I think they've died,'' he said, moving to another
alien and lifting the scarf of kyberflesh hanging from its
arm. "Or, to be more precise, that we've cut them off
from their motive force by slipping out of ordinary
lightspeed space. Yes, we've pulled their plugs. Literally, I think.''

"And when we reach Earth?''

"They'll be too far away from their power source for
any hope of resurrection. They're permanently dead,
Dr Takahashi; permanently unplugged.''

"Have you looked at their eyes, Farrell?''

"A residual glow, that's all. It'll fade. By the time
we reach Luna Port they'll all be as gloomy as candle
nubs.''

"So you no longer object to our taking them home
with us?''

"Why should I? They'll be divided up by govern-
ments and research institutes, museums and universities, and shown around like native archaeological
treasures. One or two will fall into the hands of
surgeon-mechanics for dissection and dismantling, one
or the other, choose your terminology. I don't object to
people dickering with machines, Dr Takahashi, only to
their kowtowing to them.''

"Which is what you think Andrik did?''

For the first time since entering the cargo hold,

Sixkiller seemed daunted by the uncompromising steeliness of her aspect and bearing.

"It's time—" he began gently, not meeting her gaze. "It's time you got over that, Keiko."

She ignored this. "They're alive," she defiantly told him. "They're alive, Farrell—*alive.*"

"It's time you got over that, too." He gripped her shoulders, lowering his head so that he could peer into her face searchingly. "Don't worship the dead. Don't."

"Worship you instead?"

"Or yourself, Lady Kei. Or something living."

"I will. I do." She shook free of Sixkiller's grip and brushed past him into the hold's narrow aisle. Halting, she looked back. "About which primary do you orbit these days, Farrell? Or have you contrived a way to set yourself at the centre?" Almost immediately she regretted her questions, her tone, her readiness to sacrifice Sixkiller's feelings to her own ringing anger.

"Sweet woman," he said, shaking his head and smiling. "I envied that single-minded bastard his relationship with you. It's a helluva thing, envying the dead. I still envy him."

"Shut up, Farrell." But she was staring sightlessly at the floor, and her voice conveyed no hint of reproach. She could not find the strength to move her feet. Blood pounded in her temples, and the air in the hold was suddenly stifling, unaccountably so.

When she looked up, Keiko saw that Sixkiller was inscribing a message in huge blue letters on the yellow facing of the collapsed storage balloon. His phosphor-pen moved in swift, luminous parabolas; each turn of the wrist was a hypnotic flourish.

DR TAKAHASHI, said the completed inscription, PLEASE BE MINE.

Keiko stared at it abashed and speechless, balanced between outrage and bewildered laughter. The words glowed. Momentarily even the Kybers were eclipsed by the phenomenon of Sixkiller's illuminated gallantry. Then, ceasing to gape, she allowed herself a slow, pale smile.

"Farrell—"

"It'll fade," he said resignedly. "Don't you worry, Lady Kei: it'll fade."

She shut her eyes, then opened them again, letting the inscription bleed into her vision like a sunset or a mist. "I know," she murmured. And left Farrell Sixkiller standing beside the vivid inscription, his phosphor-pen clutched tightly in one hand and a look of cynical melancholy flashing from his eyes.

A few weeks later the *Heavenbridge* was home.

TWENTY-TWO

Keiko Takahashi retired to Kyoto, where she accepted a teaching post in linguistics and forsook any ambition of going to the stars again. Her work was her life. Although she never married, for a period of three years she lived with a young man—one of her students—who hoped to revive a literary movement devoted to illuminating contemporary events in terms of ancient Japanese history and myth, and who painstakingly composed an unpublishable epic poem while sharing her apartment. Eventually, at Keiko's own insistence, the young man moved out. He later repudiated utterly the thrust and savour of his literary ambitions, accepting a low-level management post with a cryonics firm in Hiroshima.

As a form of self-mocking comment on his surrender to capitalistic paternalism, the young man made a point of sending Keiko a friendly card every April around the date of the Industrial Festival at Fushimi, during which various Japanese industrial products were ceremoniously offered to the deities. Although inflicting pain was clearly *not* their intention, these cards invariably wounded Keiko—but she always answered them faith-fully and tried, in addition, to remember the young man both on his birthday and at New Years.

The exploits of transnational expeditions to other star systems held only a peripheral interest for Keiko. She read about them in commercial news outlets or an occasional speciality journal, where colour portraits of alien landscapes would sometimes provoke disturbing reveries that she was quick to shake back down into her subconscious.

Six years after her return from Onogoro, one of these periodicals reported that Dextro, in the Gemini system, had indeed gone nova: that no further manned missions to that region of space would be undertaken, since there could be nothing there worth investigating any more—an obvious economic decision.

This report so stung Keiko that for an entire year she refrained from reading anything but her own educational materials. She had no idea what sort of command Captain Hsi had assumed after their party's demobilization at Luna Port, or where the *Heavenbridge* itself might be these days. Nor did she care.

One lovely spring, in an article about that year's recipients of the Nobel Prize in physics, Keiko encountered Craig Olivant's name. He and V.K. Mahindra had taken the award for their work on neutrino-emission interface patterns in unstable stellar binaries.

Like Captain Hsi, however, everyone else connected with the Onogoro expedition—Naomi Davis, Betti Songa, Heinrich Eshleman, Nikolai Taras, Farrell Six-killer, *everyone*–disappeared from Keiko's life as ir-revocably as if they had died thirty-seven light-years from home. They were hollow places in her past, echoes of an experience that she regarded with the same ambiguous detachment that adults often reserve for childhood nightmares.

The Kybers were another matter.

Sixkiller had been right about both their imperviousness to resurrection back on Earth and their likely fate at the hands of human researchers and curators. News about the aliens was meticulously controlled and therefore doggedly circumspect—if you cared about their disposition, which Keiko privately told herself she did not. Nevertheless, you could not escape learning that a transnational team of surgeons and cyberneticists in Houston, Texas, had dissected—dismantled—one of the Onogorovans, only to conclude that the alien represented a genuine life form, albeit a variety once powered by an enigmatic vitalism impossible to define or catagorize. The term "vitalism," which appeared in two successive news releases from the Houston hospital where the alien autopsy had taken place, came in for a great deal of sniping from medical professionals in following days; and no one, anywhere, was happy with the team's lengthy official report, to which three members refused to append their signatures. This controversy was inescapable because everyone was talking about it, even the students in Keiko's syntactical-transformation classes.

As for the other five Kybers, they disappeared altogether, the victims of Expeditionary Command reticence and red tape. In fact, it was not until an entire decade after the *Heavenbridge*'s return from the Gemini system that authorities lifted the lid on their whereabouts, revealing that within the next months the Kybers would be installed, rather like pieces of statuary, at five different public facilities around the world appropriate to their display. They would remain five years at each site, then be moved to museums, religious centres, universities, or open promenades in countries that had not yet benefited from their presence. This rotation would continue as long as there was sufficient public interest to fund and support it.

Initially, then, death-sleeping Kybers were dispatched to the Museum of Natural History in New York, the Glyptotek in Copenhagen, the Bahai Shrine in Haifa, a centre devoted to Inca culture in Lima, and the isolated rock monolith called Yakkagala on the island of Taprobane. Five years later they were dutifully rotated to other sites, and five years after that to still others, and so on.

When Keiko Takahashi was sixty-three, an alert but increasingly less nimble woman, satisfied with her career and her small circle of friends, she learned that one of the Kybers would be rotated to Sanjusangendo to stand among the thousand statues of Kannon in the Hall of Mercy.

As if her entire life had been pointing toward this development, Keiko was only mildly surprised.

More upsetting to her was the *manner* in which she acquired her knowledge of the Kyber's imminent transfer—apparently from the National Museum in Kenya—to Kyoto. She had answered a summons to her apartment door one evening to find an earnest young man with a recording unit and a finger camera standing in the hallway.

He was Japanese, quite good-looking, and he reminded Keiko of the young man whom she had inadvertently driven into the cryonics industry, and who had died several years ago in a boating accident off Akashi island near Sumoto.

"Are you Keiko Takahashi?" he asked, lifting the recorder.

She confessed her identity.

"Then you'll be interested to know . . ." And he told her about the selection of Sanjusangendo as a display site for one of the Kybers, in such pedantic detail that she was hard put not to interrupt him.

"Why would I be interested to know that?" Keiko asked the young man pointedly when he was at last finished.

"Everyone is," he replied, smiling. "Besides, you were a member of the expeditionary party aboard the *Heavenbridge*. You were one of those who brought the Kybers back from the stars."

She moved to close her door, dismayed by so direct a reference to her past, even though she had quickly surmised what was happening. That someone had taken the trouble to match her name to the manifest of her old light-skimmer and then to seek her out was nevertheless a startling discovery. Wasn't all that dead?

For a few months after the return of the *Heavenbridge* she had suffered the scrutiny of journalists and the pleas of various sorts of fortune-seekers, but the attention had died because she adamantly refused to sanction it. Later, her employers had shielded her from the press; and today, so far as she knew, the general public had no more knowledge of her name than it did of that of the first anonymous kamikaze who had given his life in the Battle of Midway . . .

"Please, Dr Takahashi," the young man cried. He had his foot in the door, just like a products salesman, and he was wedging his way inward with an apologetic smile belying the violence of his entry.

"No," Keiko declared. "Get out. Get out." She

pushed the door against his own insistent pushing, and
found that she was no match for him.

"What is especially interesting about—*ugh!*—the
timing of the Kyber's transfer to Kyoto," the young
man was telling her, still cordially grinning, "is that in
three years the nova of Dextro will be visible to Earthbound astronomers. How slowly—*umpf!*—light
travels in comparison to wonderful vessels like the
Heavenbridge, eh?"

Keiko gave up and let him in. "All right, then—
violate my home. And do so without removing your
shoes."

He looked at his feet, but only briefly.

"Know this, however," Keiko said: "I won't talk to
you, I have nothing to say."

"Is it true you taught the Kybers to speak?"

She stared at the young man contemptuously, with a
fire very like hatred in her eyes. Almost precisely when
she thought he would, he withered, turning aside to
search for some neutral household item on which to
permit his gaze to fall. He settled upon the flower
arrangement—of golden chrysanthemums—in the *tokonoma* alcove; and momentarily, with a skip of her
heart, Keiko saw there the golden heads of the haloed
statues in that other *tokonoma* holoniche in her dormicle on Onogoro so many years ago.

"Some scientists believe," he began, addressing the
flowers, "that the nova may be a—one of them calls it,
yes, a 'resurrection trigger'. If that is an accurate speculation, Dr Takahashi, the alien that comes to Sanjusangendo may awaken there. I would think that you
might have an interesting comment to make on such a
speculation."

"Then you have thought artlessly, young man."

The reporter turned to her with a rapt, committed

look reminiscent of the one unfailingly worn by her student lover of bygone years. "Don't you want to believe the Kybers are alive?" he demanded of her. "Don't you want to feel that a few of them have escaped the tragedy of their sun's misconduct?"

"Get out," said Keiko pitilessly. "Get out, please."

"You're a hard one," the young man informed her after a moment of inward struggle. "You're a terribly hard one, Dr Takahashi."

She said nothing. For a long moment he stared at her, without withering back from her gaze, then strolled to the door and let himself out. He was careful not to slam the door.

On New Year's Day, a little over three years later, the fifteenth dynastic year of the current Japanese Emperor (which is named, as is customary, not for his name in life, but for his death-name), Keiko minced painfully along Seventh Avenue—*Shichijo-dori*—towards San-jusangendo. On her back, her most gracious kimono, which she had put on for the first time since retiring from her teaching position. It clung to her snugly, silkily, like a flexible cocoon. The Hall of Mercy drew her toward it in spite of her intellectual resistance, in spite of her having told herself repeatedly that she would not cave in to so unlikely a lure.

The Hall was open every day now. Many spectators believed that the Kyber was not a dead or an inanimate organism, but merely a statue from the stars; at best, the metallic analogue of a mummy. It was not hard, Keiko thought, to sympathize with their unenlightened view of the matter. Seeking no special exemption for having once belonged to the research team assigned to the *Heavenbridge*–to have done so would have been a vile hypocrisy—she joined the tail of the serpentine queue.

It was cold inside the Hall of Mercy, barely one
degree centigrade. Keiko could not halt in front of the
Kyber because the crowd, awe-struck but implacable,
squeezed her along irresistibly. She was now one of
several hundred pilgrims actually inside the temple,
and the devotion—the scepticism—of each visitor had
to be served. As she approached, however, Keiko
studied the alien, and the fact that the astronomy unit at
Luna Port had confirmed Dextro's spectacular, though
brief, flare-up during the Occident's recent celebration
of Christmas lent her appraisal of the Kyber a quiet
excitement. She felt young again, innocent of pain and
evil and regret.

Would the Kyber, recognizing her, step down and
take her hand as she passed? Would it lift her into its
arms as she had once been lifted to the ladder of Sixkiller's floater? Would it then sprint with her from this
human crush on tireless, pistoning legs and bear her up
the hillside through the ten thousand crimson gateways
of Fushimi . . .?

Keiko watched, but the Kyber did not move.

And yet, as she was borne past the alien's pedestal,
one of its peripheral eye-bulbs seemed momentarily to
dilate, to glow, reflecting the layered gold leaf of the
neighbouring statues of Mercy.

She would come again. The promise was there.

H. BEAM PIPER

☐ 24890	**FOUR DAY PLANET/LONE STAR PLANET**	$2.25
☐ 26192	**FUZZY SAPIENS**	$1.95
☐ 48492	**LITTLE FUZZY**	$1.95
☐ 26193	**FUZZY PAPERS**	$2.75
☐ 49053	**LORD KALVAN OF OTHERWHEN**	$2.25
☐ 77779	**SPACE VIKING**	$2.25
☐ 23188	**FEDERATION (5¼'' x 8¼'')**	$5.95

ACE SCIENCE FICTION
P.O. Box 400, Kirkwood, N.Y. 13795

S-10

Please send me the titles checked above. I enclose _____.
Include 75¢ for postage and handling if one book is ordered; 50¢ per book for two to five. If six or more are ordered, postage is free. California, Illinois, New York and Tennessee residents please add sales tax.

NAME_____

ADDRESS_____

CITY_____STATE_____ZIP_____

Gordon R. Dickson

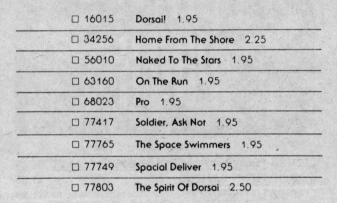

☐ 16015	Dorsai!	1.95
☐ 34256	Home From The Shore	2.25
☐ 56010	Naked To The Stars	1.95
☐ 63160	On The Run	1.95
☐ 68023	Pro	1.95
☐ 77417	Soldier, Ask Not	1.95
☐ 77765	The Space Swimmers	1.95
☐ 77749	Spacial Deliver	1.95
☐ 77803	The Spirit Of Dorsai	2.50

Available wherever paperbacks are sold or use this coupon.

ACE SCIENCE FICTION
P.O. Box 400, Kirkwood, N.Y. 13795

Please send me the titles checked above. I enclose _____ .
Include 75¢ for postage and handling if one book is ordered; 50¢ per book for two to five. If six or more are ordered, postage is free. California, Illinois, New York and Tennessee residents please add sales tax.

NAME_____

ADDRESS_____

CITY_____STATE_____ZIP_____

FRITZ LEIBER

FAFHRD AND THE GRAY MOUSER SAGA

☐ 79176	SWORDS AND DEVILTRY	$2.25
☐ 79156	SWORDS AGAINST DEATH	$2.25
☐ 79185	SWORDS IN THE MIST	$2.25
☐ 79165	SWORDS AGAINST WIZARDRY	$2.25
☐ 79223	THE SWORDS OF LANKHMAR	$1.95
☐ 79169	SWORDS AND ICE MAGIC	$2.25

Available wherever paperbacks are sold or use this coupon

ACE SCIENCE FICTION
P.O. Box 400, Kirkwood, N.Y. 13795

Please send me the titles checked above. I enclose $_____.
Include 75¢ for postage and handling if one book is ordered; $1.00 if
two to five are ordered. If six or more are ordered, postage is free.

NAME_____

ADDRESS_____

CITY_____STATE_____ZIP_____

Ursula K. Le Guin

10705	**City of Illusion** $2.25
47806	**Left Hand of Darkness** $2.25
66956	**Planet of Exile** $1.95
73294	**Rocannon's World** $1.95

Available wherever paperbacks are sold or use this coupon

ACE SCIENCE FICTION
P.O. Box 400, Kirkwood, N.Y. 13795

Please send me the titles checked above. I enclose _____.
Include 75¢ for postage and handling if one book is ordered; 50¢ per book for two to five. If six or more are ordered, postage is free. California, Illinois, New York and Tennessee residents please add sales tax.

NAME_____

ADDRESS_____

CITY_____STATE_____ZIP_____